OTHER BOOKS BY DORSEY BUTTERBAUGH

Behind Bars (with James Willey)

Trilogy In G Minor

Turtles In the Sand

M R Salisbury

The Thirteenth Headmaster

Ladies of Hatteras

THE WINDS OF BADDECK

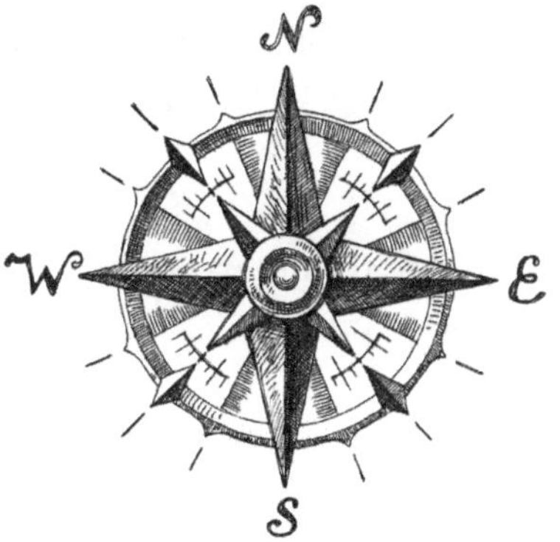

This is a work of fiction. While Baddeck and the surrounding areas are real, specific references, people, events, businesses, and the like are not.

ISBN 978-1-62806-467-4 (print | paperback)
ISBN 978-1-62806-468-1 (ebook)

Library of Congress Control Number 2025921537

Published by Salt Water Media
29 Broad Street, Suite 104
Berlin, MD 21811
www.saltwatermedia.com

Salt Water MEDIA

Cover image used with license from istockphoto.com
Interior images used with license from istockphoto.com

THE WINDS OF BADDECK

Dorsey Butterbaugh

Dedicated to my wife, Suzanne,
who suggested an anniversary trip
to the Canadian Maritime Provinces.
Little did I know…

CHAPTER 1

Early Spring
New York City

The sun bore down on the city of New York, helped by the cloudless sky. Large piles of plowed snow were rapidly reduced to dirty streams of water as Mother Nature sought to convert the weather from winter to spring. There was even some flooding in the low-lying areas. For the most part, however, vehicle and pedestrian traffic continued to crawl through the city streets. The array of buildings stood still as there was no appreciable wind. Those with glass facing the east reflected the sun's rays into unprepared eyes. Others cast shadows across the sidewalks and streets below.

One building, dwarfed and nondescript compared to most, sat two blocks off Broadway. Construction of the eight-story building began in 1930, the same year as the Empire State Building. It was financed by industrialist Richard H. Barrett, who, along with his wife, was an avid supporter of the arts. Upon his death, his wife donated the building and endowed the Barrett Conservatory of Music. While the interior of the building had been redesigned and modernized over the years, the external facade of stone remained the same. As the school's reputation grew, BCM was now considered one of the top music conservatories in the world.

On this particular morning, you could hear a variety of musical instruments from the practice studios as students worked to master their most recent assignment. On the eighth floor, in Studio 888, sat a Steinway piano, one of four full grand pianos in the building. This one, named Beauty by the students, was considered the best because of the quality of its touch and tone. Studio 888 was also the classroom used exclusively by Dr. Joseph Cunningham, professor of piano performance, nicknamed the Beast.

Dr. Cunningham had been pacing for the past thirty minutes as he listened to the piece being played. Now he sat in one of the chairs, his head back, eyes closed, an arm across his forehead. He was a robust tall man in his early sixties with shoulder length gray hair, currently pulled back in a ponytail. His lips were puckered out somewhat. His facial expression was intense. As he rose to his feet, he walked over to the Steinway, he leaned forward and sought to make eye contact with the young man sitting at the piano.

Twenty-four-year-old Jason Kinde was six foot two inches with long arms and long fingers. His nails were carefully manicured. Thanks to a rigorous physical training schedule of runs through Central Park and visits to the gym in the building where he lived, he was well built and rather muscular. His jet-black hair was full. It had been neatly combed initially, but as so often was the case when he played, it now sat disarrayed atop his head. He approached his study of the piano with the unrivaled intensity and highly structured lifestyle necessary to become one of the world's elite concert pianists.

He sat with his head bowed, eyes closed. His breathing

was hard, and he wore a painful and angry expression. After a couple of deep breaths, he looked up, fully expecting the cave of the Beast's mouth to explode with wild verbiage.

The words came with intensity, yet much softer in tone than expected. "Jason… Jason… Jason," Dr. Cunningham started. "How long have you been playing the piano? Since you were five?"

"About four," the pupil corrected.

"Four, then." A brief pause ensued. "And since the ripe age of four, you have developed into one of the premiere young pianists, not only at BCM, not only in this city, this country, but in the world. You have won, or come close to winning, every competition you've entered since you've been here. Your poise, your technical skills, your ability to learn new works quickly, are unsurpassed. You are on track to become one of the best, if not the best pianist this school has ever produced…and yes, better than me."

An alum of BCM, Joseph Cunningham's rise as a concert pianist upon graduating was rapid. He played with symphonies and in venues all over the world, but his career was cut short by a heart attack in his late thirties. He survived, quit smoking, and returned to his alma mater to devote his talents to the teaching of others. That was twenty years ago. He had since become one of the most sought-after instructors at the school.

"But you know all that, don't you, Jason?" the professor continued. He didn't wait for an answer. "Sure, you do. You've been told that since you were old enough to understand the concept. While technically superb, your play at times is raw and aggressive. It's like you're fucking the piano rather than making love to it."

Dr. Cunningham looked away. His voice softened. "You know, Jason, I had a close friend when I was growing up named Randy Burns. My passion in life was music. His was mountain climbing. He liked to tell me that above a certain elevation, for every foot you climb, the danger of not making it down alive increases significantly.

"We were having dinner together one evening after I'd returned from an especially grueling performance schedule. Randy could see that I was exhausted. He said that one should never try and summit when you are so tired you can't enjoy the experience. He also told me that climbers conquered this difficulty through what he termed acclimating to the altitude."

"What's that have to do with me?" Jason demanded.

"You're climbing too fast without proper acclimation. You need to slow up and take a deep breath. Your life is so controlled, so focused, all you see is the summit. This puts you on a dangerous path. I want you to make love to the piano, not treat it like something to be conquered."

The professor paused briefly. "You need to acclimate, Jason. You need a change...a change of venue."

. . . . .

Jason took the stairs as usual down the eight flights, crossed the lobby, and pushed through the heavy doors to the outside. His mind was in a fog, thinking about the years he'd spent studying at BCM, the last three under Dr. Cunningham. While the man was a phenomenal teacher, his potential for harshness was well known. A young pianist had to learn that the key to survival was to become as hard on oneself as the Beast would be. As such, Jason developed an internal drive, setting high expectations for his musical studies and performance as well as other aspects of his life.

The present fog had developed because this was the first time Dr. Cunningham had not behaved as usual and had not focused solely on Jason's playing; instead, he'd talked about Jason the person.

"I'm climbing the mountain too fast?" Jason mouthed. "Isn't that what BCM expects?" Chilled by the outside air, he pulled the coat collar around his neck. "Acclimate?" The most concerning part, however, was the comment about him needing a change.

He made his way across the street and headed toward his building. A hard work out in the basement gym followed by a run in the park would help clear his mind.

CHAPTER 2

The ringing of the phone startled the old man out of a deep sleep. He shook his head to fully wake up as he pulled his recliner to the upright position. He grabbed his glasses and cell phone from the side table. A smile crossed his face when he saw the name of the caller.

"Joseph, my friend!" he said. "So happy to hear from you, but it's not the beginning of the month." The caller was one of his oldest friends, Joseph Cunningham.

"No, it's not the beginning of the month, Andrew… Uncle Andy," Cunningham said, referring to their monthly calls to one another.

Andrew laughed. "I see you're finally learning how to properly address this old man."

Dr. Cunningham chuckled. "For one, Andrew, you're not old. For another…." He let the thought fade away, not wanting the conversation to go down that path. "How are you doing, my friend?"

"No different than when we talked a few weeks ago. And you?"

"Good," the professor said.

Uncle Andy took a sip of water sitting on the table. "What can I do for you?"

"I need a favor."

"I'm listening."

And so, Uncle Andy listened for the next few minutes.

. . . . .

Laura Kinde grabbed her robe from the back of the bathroom door, wrapped her hair in a towel and made her way down the hallway to the kitchen. There she made a cup of tea and grabbed an apple from the counter. It would hold her over until dinner later in the evening. Dinner with clients, the third such event this week. She let out a soft chuckle.

"Don't complain," she said aloud. "Clients buying our gowns and accessories is what keeps us in business." She worked as an associate for her mother's firm, Kinde's House of Fashion and Design and was becoming one of the most popular young fashion designers in the city.

She looked out from the floor-to-ceiling windows in the kitchen. The view overlooking Central Park was magnificent as always from their apartment in Manhattan. It had been even more sensational during the last snowstorm. She took a bite of apple as she made her way down the hallway through the apartment she shared with her twin brother, Jason. It was spacious, contemporarily decorated, and immaculately kept. The twins cared for their apartment with the same strict structure and discipline that they applied to their lives.

Both brother and sister were attractive, with their raven-black hair, fair skin, and green eyes. Both were tall and thin, Laura with a willowy beauty including full, reddish lips, Jason with a muscular build that had developed as he came out of his teens. In previous years, both Laura and Jason had served as models for their mother. Good-looking twins in the fashion industry were usually a hit. Laura still served in that capacity on occasion, but much preferred being the designer. Jason had given up the fashion runway to focus on his music.

Laura paused at a full-length mirror, one of the mirrors strategically placed to give the penthouse a larger appearance. She tightened the belt on her bathrobe and turned in a circle, pretending to model one of her newest creations. She had several in the works, but the newest, a full-length blue satin gown, was proving to be her favorite. Its beauty was in its simplicity. It had a shoulder strap on the left side and was cut low in the back and in the front—although *how* low was decided by the client, since each gown was custom-fitted.

She loosened the belt so she could take a better gander at herself. She had been fortunate that both her parents passed along their genes of thinness. A strict yet healthy diet, plus frequent visits to her personnel trainer did the rest. She saw no flaws and was covering herself up when her cellphone started ringing. She hurried back to the kitchen where she had left it on the counter. She tapped the speaker button without looking at the screen. "Hello," she said.

"Laura…Ms. Kinde?"

"This is she."

"Hello. This is Joseph Cunningham."

"Dr. Cunningham! It's been a long time. How are you doing?" she said, readjusting her bathrobe.

"I'm fine. Thanks for asking. How are you and your parents?"

"Everyone's okay. Mother's been in Paris this week getting

ready for an upcoming show. Father's been holed up in his office downtown working on heaven only knows what." Laura paused briefly. "If you're calling to speak to my brother, he's not home yet. He should be …." She stopped suddenly. "Why are you calling on my number if you want Jason?"

Dr. Cunningham gave a nervous cough. "I called because it's you I want to speak with…about your brother, that is."

"Is Jason okay?"

"Yes…yes. Didn't mean to startle you. He's fine."

"Okay, then. What can I do for you?"

The professor started. "Let me say that Jason has on more than one occasion talked about you being the foundation that keeps him upright. He calls you his lifeline to sanity. He says you two have a very close relationship."

Laura laughed. "To be honest, I think he does as much for me as I do for him."

Laura didn't go into the reasons behind that. Their parents had always been loving and provided them with anything they could want, but parenting had become more of a long-distance affair as she and her brother grew older. As the design business grew, their mother spent more and more time traveling. Their father, while only several miles away, was buried for long hours in his office on Wall Street. He was an expert financial analyst in foreign stock exchanges; his business hours were simply defined as *whenever*.

"Anyway," Laura continued, "what's going on?"

"I'm worried about Jason."

"I worry about him every day," Laura quipped. "What's different today?"

The professor answered quickly. "As you know, Jason is internally driven. The pressures placed on students at the conservatory only add to that stress." Sighing, Cunningham continued. "You brother is one of the most talented pianists I have ever encountered. His progress since coming to us has been amazing. My reason for wanting to talk to you is that I'm concerned he is at risk of collapsing because of this intensity."

"In other words, burning out," Laura suggested.

"Yes."

Laura took a moment to digest what she'd heard. She took it upon herself to keep a watchful eye on her brother's physical and emotional well-being. Sure, he was high-strung and focused on becoming one of the world's finest pianists. Whenever she heard him play, which was often as they had a baby grand Steinway in their penthouse, she thought he played wonderfully, although she did admit a certain amount of prejudice.

Aloud, she asked, "Why the concern now?"

"Technically, there's no one at the conservatory that comes close to Jason," Dr. Cunningham said. "However, there's more to performing the classics than reading and playing the notes on the paper. There's a need to…." He paused to clarify his thoughts. "To paraphrase an analogy given to me by a previous instructor, your brother plays like he's … like he's having raw sex, when he should be making love to a beautiful woman."

Laura's eyes widened, which she was glad the professor could not see. "I appreciate your candor," she said with a chuckle.

Dr. Cunningham continued quickly. "Adding beauty to the performance is what makes one stand out, regardless the type of music or the instrument being played."

"Do you have a solution?" Laura asked.

"I do."

. . . . .

When the call ended, Laura spent a minute staring at the cellphone's screen. She'd had a few previous conversations with Joseph Cunningham over the years, usually at a recital or other social setting. She always thought the man, while cordial, a bit aloof, although, he always had positive things to say about Jason. This afternoon on the phone, he was different, definitely not living up to his reputation as the Beast. He'd voiced genuine concern for Jason the person, not just the piano prodigy.

Her thoughts were interrupted when Jason came through the door, entering in his usual loud and fast manner. He slid to a stop when he saw his twin sister standing in front of the mirror.

"I suspect the cost of seeing perfection is priceless," he said.

Laura tipped her head to the side. "I'll take that as a compliment, so thank you." She closed the distance to her brother and gave him a light hug followed by a kiss on the cheek. "How was your day?" Noticing his sweaty hair, she added, "I see you've already been to the gym."

"The *gym* was fine. I had a good work out and a run afterwards."

Noting that her brother emphasized the word gym and did not mention his studio lesson, Laura said, "What about the rest of your day?"

"We can talk about that later. I know you have a date tonight," he replied.

"It's not a date! I'm meeting with some…" Laura stopped. "Nice try at deflecting the conversation. Go take a shower – you smell – then we can talk."

Jason tipped his head to the side. "Why the urgency?"

Laura hesitated. "I just got off the phone with Dr. Cunningham."

"What did he want?" Jason said with surprise.

Laura motioned him away. "Shower first."

When he came out a few minutes later, Laura was sitting in the great room staring out the window. She was now dressed in jeans and a plain red tee shirt. He had dressed similarly. He grabbed a bottle of water from the kitchen and plopped down in the love seat across from her.

After taking a long swallow of the water, he said, "Okay what's up?"

When they were in their early teens, the twins made a pact to always talk openly about issues they might have. "No *fluffy words*," Laura had said at the time. The pact served them well over the years. Laura looked her brother in the eye.

"Like I said, Dr. Cunningham called a short time ago. He thinks you're on the verge of crashing and burning. He thinks you're too focused on your music."

"He mentioned that to me," Jason said nonchalantly, taking another swallow of water.

"*Mentioned* that?"

"Okay, more than mentioned. He used the analogy of how I was having sex with the piano," Jason said. He paused for a moment. "I assume he didn't mince words with you either."

His sister laughed. "He made his point."

"He said he had an idea he wanted to think about," Jason said. "Did he say anything about that to you?"

Laura hesitated. "He thinks you need to get away for a while."

"You mean leave the city?"

"That's part of it."

"But I'm preparing for my masters recital. I need that to graduate," Jason pointed out.

"That's what, seven months away?" Laura countered. "You'll still be able to practice, just not in as intense an environment. He's also arranged for you to work with someone while you're away."

"Is this a done deal?" Jason snapped. "Don't I have a say?"

"Yes, you have a say, Jason," Laura countered. "It's your life." Laura knew her brother would withdraw emotionally if she came across as too demanding. She took a deep breath. "Listen, Jason, except for a couple of papers, you've completed all your class work for your masters. The only thing left is your recital. Writing the papers and preparation for the recital can be done anywhere."

"So, you're sending me *away*," Jason pouted.

"No one is *sending* you anywhere, Jason. You have to be willing to do this."

Jason glanced out the window. Darkness was now engulfing the city as streetlights and the lights in the park were flickering on. *Symbolic*, Jason thought. Aloud, "What do Mom and Dad think?"

"I haven't talked to them yet, but I will. I'm sure they'll agree to whatever Dr. Cunningham suggests, as long as you agree, of course."

"Going anywhere for that long of time is going to be expensive," Jason said, thinking that might be a way to get out of whatever they had planned.

Laura tipped her head to the side. "Jason…"

"Yeah, I know," Jason interrupted. "Mom and Dad will support me anyway needed."

He agreed with everything Cunningham had said earlier. Actually, the thought of burning out had been brewing in his own mind for months; he had just been denying it.

"Who's the person I'll be working with?" he said aloud.

"All Dr. Cunningham would say was he went by Uncle Andy."

"Uncle Andy? Who the hell is that?"

"I haven't a clue."

"Where is he sending me, anyway?"

"A town called Baddeck. That's in Nova Scotia."

CHAPTER 3

Three weeks later
Halifax, Nova Scotia

The bumping and screeching of tires on the runway woke Jason from a sound sleep. He remembered taking off from LaGuardia; otherwise, he recalled nothing until now. He sat up as he ran a hand through his hair. He looked out the window and saw the sky was cloudy, but there was no rain, although it had been predicted. He watched until they pulled up to the gate. He grabbed his carry-on from the overhead compartment and waited to exit the plane.

He cleared customs without difficulty, stating the reason for his visit to Canada was study and vacation. After collecting his luggage, he followed the signs to the exit. He pulled a piece of paper from his pocket...*Baddeck...a hundred seventy miles from Halifax.* He had done no other research on the area, figuring if he was going to go on an adventure, he might as well make it as adventurous as possible. The mileage was simply to get a feel for how far he had left to travel once the plane landed.

Walking through the airport lobby, Jason saw a tall, thin, elderly man dressed in a sports shirt and khaki shorts holding a place card with his name on it. Jason went up and introduced himself. As they shook hands, Jason noticed the man spoke with a strong accent he was unable to place.

"Mr. Kinde, it's a pleasure to meet you," the man said. "I'm Alex. I'm the maintenance director for Baddeck Cottage. I also drive when called upon. If you'll come with me, please." Alex grabbed the two suitcases and headed toward the exit.

"I didn't know the hotel was sending a car. I was expecting to get a taxi," Jason said, pulling the strap from the carry-on over his left shoulder.

"I needed to come to Halifax today to pick up some plumbing parts and other supplies," Alex explained. "So, Gabbey asked me to stop and pick you up as well. It'll save you a pile of change." He let out a chuckle as he added, "Plus, you can help me with the supplies."

Jason said nothing as they headed toward short-term parking where they loaded Jason's luggage into the back of a white multi-passenger van with a picture and logo of Baddeck Cottage on the side panels.

They exited the airport complex and merged onto a four-lane highway. Jason sat back and took in the scenery. He noted how the countryside was farmland mixed in with forested areas. Everything looked well-kept, almost picture-perfect in Jason's mind, although he didn't have anything to compare it with. His out-of-the-city travels usually started at one of the New York airports and ended at another big city airport as he followed piano competitions around the world.

After a few miles, or rather kilometers, Jason said, "Where are we stopping for supplies?"

"Walmart," Alex answered.

"Walmart ... You're kidding?"

"I take it you've never been here before?" Alex said.

"Never been to Canada, actually," Jason acknowledged.

"There's a lot of history in this part of Canada, and a lot to see." When Jason remained silent, Alex continued, "What brings you here anyway?"

Jason spoke as he looked out the passenger window. "I'm a music student and have to prepare for a recital and write a couple papers before I graduate. The people around me feel I need to get away from the rigors of my program and the city."

"The pressures to succeed, eh," Alex said. "Sometimes pressure is good, but if it gets too great and the lid blows off the pot, it can make a mess all over the kitchen." The man let out a soft chuckle. "My wife, Maria, who you will meet soon, works at the Cottage as well. She relates a lot of things to food."

"I look forward to meeting her," Jason said. Wanting to deflect further personal questions, he asked, "Where are you from originally?"

"My wife and I immigrated here from Ukraine fifteen years ago. I was an electrical engineer, and my wife was a schoolteacher. We retired and didn't like what we saw for the future, so we left. We traveled through Europe, then to various places in the States. When we came to Canada on a bus trip, we never left." He paused, focusing on the traffic for a moment before continuing. "Hopefully, you'll get to experience the hospitality and beauty of Canada ... without a lot of pressure."

Jason let out a huff of air. "That would be nice."

A short time after entering the outskirts of Halifax, they pulled into the parking lot of a Walmart. They made their way to the back where there was a large pallet of supplies waiting for them on the loading dock.

Helping Alex load the van, Jason said, "They don't do deliveries where we're going?"

"We have UPS and all those other services, but sometimes it's more efficient to do it this way. Besides, we needed a few plumbing supplies ASAP."

With Jason's help, they were loaded and on their way in less than twenty minutes. As they made their way through the city, Alex pointed out the cemetery where many victims of the *Titanic* were buried, explaining that the people of Halifax were some of the first rescuers to arrive on scene of the disaster.

"There's a boardwalk covering part of the waterfront," Alex explained. "There's a variety of restaurants, hotels, and shops geared toward the tourists. I often stop to get a bite to eat and an ice cream, but the weather is supposed to get worse later, so I want to keep rolling."

A short time later, Alex pointed out the site in the harbor where in 1917 two ships collided and caught fire, igniting three thousand tons of munitions and explosives that one of them was carrying. "Seventeen hundred lives were lost; over nine thousand injured," Alex narrated. "The property destruction was catastrophic."

"I was in New York City the morning of 9/11," Jason said. "My father works on Wall Street. Luckily, he hadn't gotten to the office yet." Jason remembered the morning as if it was yesterday. It was the longest hour of his life, almost sixty minutes before his father was able to call home to let everyone know he was okay. While Jason himself didn't know anyone who perished, his father knew many.

"One never knows, do they?" Alex commented.

They made their way across the harbor and out of the city. Halifax was a much larger city than Jason anticipated, making him wonder what other surprises were in store for him. A short time later, they merged onto a two-lane highway. Leaning against the door, Jason was soon asleep.

CHAPTER 4

Baddeck, Nova Scotia

Baddeck Cottage came into view as Alex drove the van up the driveway. The complex sat at the base of the Cape Breton Highlands on the highest elevation in town. Gravel pathways weaved their way through gardens filled with an array of early spring flowers. Several ponds and fountains were in the mix as well. The main building was white with brown-shuttered windows that gave the appearance of a grand Swiss chalet. The steep, black, slate roof was designed to shed snow. Alex pointed out several other buildings tucked in the back, including staff housing and storage. One building was a long, rectangular structure, metal frame and glass, which contained an indoor pool and fitness center.

Alex backed the van up to one of the storage buildings. Shutting off the engine, he said, “Lunch break’s over. Time to get back to work.”

Jason laughed and followed the man’s lead.

When the van was nearly emptied, a woman of about fifty came around the corner. She was short, stocky, and dressed in jeans and a red polo top with the cottage’s logo across the front. Her long, blond hair was pulled back in a ponytail. Her head was bare, but she had a wide-brimmed wicker gardening hat in her left hand. She was wiping her forehead with a handkerchief held in her right. Her round face was somewhat weathered. She had a bright smile accentuated by a small gap in her upper teeth. Her hands were covered in gardening gloves; her jeans were tucked into a pair of rubber boots.

She did a quick look at what was going on and said, "Where'd you get the help, Alex?"

Alex motioned to Jason as he said, "Found him at the airport."

The woman moved toward Jason. Removing her gloves, she held out a hand, "Gabrielle Summers, resident gardener. You can call me Gabbey."

Jason sat the box down he had been holding and took the hand. "Jason Kinde. Resident van unloader. Nice to meet you, Ms. Summers ... Gabbey."

The woman turned her attention back to Alex. Half-teasing, half-serious, she said, "Since when do you make our guests work?"

Picking the box back up, Jason spoke. "I volunteered, Gabbey." He headed into the garage with his load. Looking over his shoulder, he added, "Alex said I'd have to ride up on the roof if I didn't."

Gabbey laughed as she shook her head. "When you finish volunteering here, Jason, drop your bags at the registration desk. Someone will get them upstairs for you. Then stop by my office; it's to the left as you walk in the main entrance. We'll get you situated. Until then...." She looked at the pile of supplies. "Thanks for your help." She turned and headed back the way she had come.

Jason came back to the van and watched her turn the corner. "And she is…?"

"The owner," Alex said. "The Baddeck Cottage has been in her family for several generations."

"Interesting lady," Jason said, as he pulled another box from the van.

. . . . .

Alex pulled the vehicle around to the front so Jason could register and take his luggage inside. The lobby was bright with the registration desk in the far-left corner. Rustic couches, chairs, and tables were set around, giving guests space to sit and talk. A full-service bar, lounge, and main dining room were to the right. Offices were down a hallway on the left. Signage pointed to a series of banquet/conference rooms in the back. The floor was covered in marble tiles with accent rugs depicting various scenes of the region. The walls were decorated with paintings and photographs by local artists and lit for easy observation. The atmosphere left Jason with a warm, comfortable feeling. It was different than what he was used to back home, where most décor seemed to be *modern chic*.

A cute, short, petite blonde girl was working behind the registration desk.

"I'm here to check in and see Gabbey," Jason said with a smile.

"Name, please?" she chirped with her own smile.

"Jason Kinde."

The girl's smile widened. Her vocal tone remained the same. "Welcome to Baddeck Cottage, Mr. Kinde. We've been expecting you. I hope your trip was pleasant."

"I slept most of the flight from New York," Jason admitted.

When the girl finished Jason's registration, she pointed to her left. "Gabbey's office is the last one down the hall."

Jason wasn't sure what he expected of the owner's office of a chateau in rural Canada. What he found was a spacious room with floor-to-ceiling windows on three walls giving a panoramic view of most of the property. Furnishings were rustic with a variety of plants spread around the room.

Gabbey had changed into khaki slacks and a red polo shirt. She gestured for Jason to take a seat.

"Let me officially welcome you to Baddeck Cottage. I trust your time here will be enjoyable. I so enjoyed speaking with your older sister when she called to arrange your stay."

Jason let out a soft chuckle. "She said she was my older sister?"

"That's not true?"

Jason laughed again. "Oh, it's true, by three minutes."

Gabbey stared blankly for a moment before smiling. "Twins, eh?"

Jason nodded.

"She did seem overly protective and concerned."

"She and everyone else," Jason ventured. He continued after a brief pause. "Did she tell you anything about why I'm here?"

"She said you're a gifted pianist finishing your masters

degree in music," Gabbey replied. "You have a couple of papers to write and have to prepare for your final recital."

"Speaking of which, my professor was supposed to arrange for me to work with someone nearby. I thought that a little strange, being so far…" Jason hesitated.

"Out in the boonies," Gabbey suggested with a grin.

Jason blushed slightly.

Gabbey quickly continued. "I suspect you are going to experience some culture shock, you coming from a big city and all that." She paused briefly. "I've spoken to Uncle Andy. He's going to meet with you as soon as he gets back in town."

"Uncle Andy?"

Gabbey's grin expanded to a smile. "He should be back in a day or so." She opened a folder on her cluttered desk. "We've given you a suite on the top floor with a small kitchenette. It has a view on three sides, much like this office. The floor is only used for special occasions and overflow, so it should be quiet."

Looking at the potted plants," Jason said, "I've never been a big flower person. It might be nice to have a few sitting around. If nothing else, they smell good."

"I can send a few pots up, if you'd like."

Jason nodded. "I'd like that." He wasn't sure why he said that except the fragrances were pleasant.

"Anyway, you're paid up for the season," Gabbey said. "You can use the pool and fitness center next to it. There's a complimentary breakfast each morning. Dinner is available from four to eight each evening. Lite fare is available in the bar and lounge area after that. If there's anything special you need, let us know." The cottage owner rose to her feet. "Your luggage should be upstairs by now. I suggest you familiarize yourself by walking around the grounds and the town as well. I think you'll find the area quite beautiful. Winter when it snows, is postcard-perfect as well."

"I think I'll go to my room and rest a bit, then walk around."

Gabbey nodded. "Just be aware of moose or bears. They can be quite intimidating, eh."

"What do I do if I come across one?" Jason said, unable to hide the concern in his voice.

"Keep a sharp eye out, and if visibility is poor, like in the woods, sing or talk so they know where you are and can avoid you. If you do see one, calmly walk away. Give it space," Gabbey said. "Now go on out to the front desk. Someone there will show you to your room."

Jason started to walk away when he remembered to ask, "My sister said you have a piano on site?"

"That we do," Gabbey said. "I'm not sure where it is right now, probably in one of the conference rooms. We use it mostly for weddings and special occasions. We have a big Christmas Holiday party here as well and hire someone to play, that is if we can find anyone. Not too many pianists in the area. Ask one of the staff. If they don't know where it is, they'll find it. It's yours to use as you please." She paused and glanced away. "It's been a long time since I've heard it played up to its potential. Maybe you can change that, eh?"

Jason shuttered at the image of an old, run-down piano stuffed in the back corner somewhere. "I'll try my best," he said.

. . . . .

Jason found Alex at the front desk, chatting with the cute, blonde receptionist. The maintenance supervisor saw him and asked if he was getting settled in okay.

"So far, thanks," Jason answered. "I was just talking to Gabbey. She said someone would show me to my room."

"Your luggage is already up there, Mr. Kinde," the girl said.

"Jason is fine," Jason said.

"Okay, Mr. Jason."

Jason started to speak when Alex cut him off. "Cindy is new here. She's doing an internship for school while she's continuing classes online. If she likes it, she may sign on full-time. Right, Cindy?"

"I'm studying hotel management," Cindy answered. "This seems like a good place to get some experience."

"She'd done well so far," Alex said. "If you have any questions or there's anything you need, just ask Cindy, or one of the other front desk girls."

"Sounds good," Jason said, nodding thanks.

"Anyway, come on," Alex said. "I'll show you your room. Besides, we just opened it up yesterday and turned on the air conditioning unit. I want to make sure everything is working."

Jason again nodded to Cindy and then turned to Alex. "Lead the way."

The suite was everything Gabbey promised and more.

There was a bedroom with two queen-size beds. A large flat screen TV was mounted on the far wall. There was a small sitting room with another TV and a kitchenette with all the standard appliances. The bathroom was large with a walk-in shower. The décor throughout was upscale with a rustic flare.

His two suitcases and carry-on were set up on luggage racks. After Alex checked everything and left, Jason contemplated unpacking but decided instead to lay down for a few minutes. The bed was comfortable. The mattress was perfect. He fell asleep almost immediately.

CHAPTER 5

Jason awoke with a start, confused at first where he was. Rubbing the sleep from his eyes, he stood up, stretched, and looked outside. The sun was setting with a glimmer of light left in the sky. He noticed the ground was dry, so it had yet to rain. A glance at the clock on the bedside table told him that if he hurried, he had time to get to dinner. He took a quick shower, changed clothes, and headed toward the elevator.

Seeing it was close to closing time for the dining room, he decided to check out the lounge area, which was basically an extension of the dining room. There were several people, mostly couples, sitting at the bar. Jason took a seat at the far end where he could take in the surroundings. He didn't have any hobbies per say, but he liked to people-watch. New York City was a great place for that. He figured rural Canada would be a good spot as well. Working out a kink in his back, he made a mental note to check out the pool and fitness area first thing in the morning. His muscles weren't used to this lack of activity and were letting him know it.

Looking around, he took in the relaxed environment. He watched an elderly foursome at a table across the dining room. They were laughing as if someone had just told a joke. Glasses were raised and a toast made. He guessed they were here on vacation and didn't have a worry in the world. He tried to relax as well but couldn't help thinking what was he doing here? He should be....

He cut the thought off. He promised his sister he would keep an open mind, and so he would.

The bartender approached. He looked to be in his late thirties, about five eight and very fit-looking. His facial features were hard, but he had a friendly smile. His dirty blond hair was pulled in a ponytail that hung down to his shoulders. He wore the standard bartender uniform of a white shirt, black vest, and black pants. "Evening. I'm Bobby. What can I get you?"

Jason scanned the array of beer taps and bottles of liquor on the back shelves. He seldom drank alcohol but decided he'd celebrate tonight and have something. Focusing on the beer taps, he saw none that he recognized. Pointing toward them, he said, "Which of those do you recommend?"

"You new to the area?"

"Is it that obvious?" Jason said, somewhat defensively.

"Most people around here are," Bobby said with a laugh. When he finished wiping the area in front of Jason, he set five coasters, making sure they were spaced and lined up neatly. "We offer a flight, a sampler of five four-ounce beers. You can pick or I'll chose for you."

"You chose," Jason said, liking the idea of a sampling. "I'll need something to eat with that though."

Bobby glanced at his watch. "You still have time to order off the main menu. If you want a recommendation there, I like the fish and chips."

"Sounds good," Jason said with a nod. He normally

avoided fried food but again decided to splurge and try something different.

The flight of beer was a good recommendation. After a taste of each, he decided he liked the lighter side of the flight better. The food was good as well. The fish was thinly battered and not greasy. He especially liked the coleslaw that came as a side.

The crowd thinned out as the evening progressed. Jason looked at his watch and saw it was getting close to closing so he motioned to Bobby for his check.

"Gabbey told me there's a piano here somewhere," Jason said while signing the bill to his room. "Happen to know where it is?"

Bobby took the signed receipt with one hand. With the other, he motioned toward the far corner of the lounge area. "It's over there in the corner. Don't know why, but someone brought it over before I got here. It's covered, so you probably didn't notice it."

Jason looked in the direction Bobby pointed. The bartender had been right; he hadn't noticed it.

"You play?" Bobby asked.

"Sometimes." Jason's hesitation didn't go unnoticed.

"It hasn't been played in a while," Bobby said. "Gabbey always wanted to have a piano bar, but there are very few pianists in the area. We use it mainly for weddings and things like that."

"Can I have a look?" Jason said.

Bobby took a couple steps to his left. He reached up to an electrical panel and hit a switch. A series of ceiling lights came on over the area.

Jason slid off the bar stool and walked over to the area. He saw it was a baby grand-sized instrument. There were a couple decorative pots filled with spring flowers sitting on top of the cover. He carefully set them on the floor. He stepped around to the keyboard side and unzipped the cover. The image of an old worn-out instrument returned. Carefully lifting the material, he exposed the front. Except for a few marks, the black wood was brightly polished. He folded the cover back another couple feet until he could see the words *Steinway and Sons* stenciled on the side. He looked skyward and mouthed a silent thank you. He sat down and closed his eyes. It was his normal routine before he started playing.

Hands poised above the keys, he was about to start a set of scales when a voice interrupted him. "I see you found it."

He saw Gabbey standing off to the side.

"Evening," he said. "Bobby said it was okay to have a look."

"No problem," Gabbey said. "I had 'em move it here for you earlier. Don't know if it's in tune or not."

Jason hesitated. Looking at his watch as an excuse, he said, "It's getting late, and Bobby wants to close up. I'll check it out in the morning." He was eager to play, but concerned the instrument was as out of tune as he suspected.

"We close to the public at ten, but some of the staff usually hang around for a drink or two." She let out a chuckle. "We had a few young people staying here last week who wanted to know where the late-night bar was in town. I told them they were sitting at it. During the season on Fridays and the weekends, we often get local workers coming up here after their places close. We stay open if the crowd's big enough."

Jason refocused on the piano, deciding to give it a go. Positioning his hands over the lower register. He played a series of scales up the keyboard. There were a couple sticky keys which he was able to work lose with repetitive strikes. While indeed out of tune, the instrument still had a beautiful tone. Then again, it was a Steinway, and Jason would have expected nothing less.

When he stopped, Gabbey stood quietly for a few seconds before she spoke. "I don't know what that was, but it was beautiful."

"I'll second that," Bobby said from behind the bar.

Jason looked at them and smiled. "It was just some scales to warm up with…and to see how it sounds."

"Sounded great to me," Gabbey reiterated.

"Couple keys are sticky," Jason said. He struck a couple more keys. "When's the last time it was tuned?"

Gabbey let out a huff of air. "It's never been tuned that I know of. There's no one around here to do that."

"I'll see what I can do," Jason said with a smirk.

Gabbey tipped her head to the side. "Don't tell me…"

"It'll be our secret," Jason said. He pulled the lid over the keys. "Mind if I keep the cover off so it can breathe overnight."

"I didn't know pianos breathed. Sure, go ahead," Gabbey said.

"THAT's the noise I hear coming from the back when it's quiet around here," Bobby said dramatically. "Damn thing's trying to get a breath under the cover."

Gabbey laughed. Jason shook his head side to side.

It was a night to have a good laugh, something he hadn't had in a while.

. . . . .

Jason went up to his room, which was at the end of the hall on the top floor. Alex had told him this floor was all suites, which were seldom booked except for weddings and overflow. Jason didn't mind as he was looking forward to some peace and quiet. At the same time, he wondered if he was going to miss the sounds of the city.

He brushed his teeth and laid across the bed, telling himself he'd rest a minute before undressing. He awoke the next morning when a beam of sunlight came in through the shades he hadn't closed. He was still fully dressed and still atop the covers. He felt well rested and relaxed; something he had not experienced recently.

A glance at the clock told him it was almost 7:00 am. He thought about going for a run, but nixed the idea, remembering he didn't know the area and keeping in mind the warnings about wildlife. Besides, he was anxious to go downstairs and have a closer look at the piano. After showering and dressing, he pulled a small leather case from his carry-on bag and headed out the door.

The breakfast buffet was up and running with several guests already in line. He thought about eating but decided he could wait. He made his way to the lounge, which was closed off. The lights were dimmed and, except for the faint wind chimes-like clinking of silverware against dishes, the area was quiet.

He took a deep breath and muttered, "Peace and quiet."

He sat down at the piano and adjusted the seat. He played some scales similar to the night before. "Ugh," he muttered. He unwrapped the leather case and went to work.

. . . . .

Ninety or so minutes later, Gabbey came out of the kitchen to see how breakfast was going. She walked around, speaking to several guests, asking how they were enjoying their stay. Everyone seemed pleased, which pleased her, since she had prepared the breakfast as the regular breakfast cook had the day off. She was at a table talking to a middle-aged couple from California when she stopped mid-sentence. Someone was playing the piano.

The man at the table noticed her reaction and spoke up. "We've been hearing that, too. Sounds like someone is tuning a piano."

Gabbey excused herself and headed toward the lounge area.

The lights were off, but there was enough ambient light to see Jason sitting on the bench. One hand was on the keyboard, the other arm draped over the top, his hand somewhere inside the instrument. She noticed several tools sitting beside him.

He looked up as he sensed her approach. "Morning," he said.

"Morning," Gabbey replied pleasantly but with concern in her voice. "I thought you were joking last night when you said you could tune this."

"I'm not a certified piano tuner, but I thought I'd give it a try. Plus, I wanted to fix the keys that were sticking."

"You did that, too?"

Jason played a couple scales with his free hand. "So far, so good."

"What's this going to cost me?" Gabbey said, trying to hide the concern from her voice.

Jason sat up straight. "Like I said, I'm not certified, and even if I was, I wouldn't charge you. Last night was the best night's sleep I've had in ages. That's payment enough."

Gabbey worked hard to hide her relief. While she was generous with staff salaries and quick to okay needed maintenance and upgrade issues regarding the facility, she was thrifty with expenses that she thought unnecessary, including a seldom-used piano.

"I'm glad you slept well," she said. "Hopefully, that will continue."

"I'm about finished," Jason said. He played a series of scales and chords. "Sound better?"

Gabbey was impressed and told him so.

"I hope I didn't bother anyone at breakfast," Jason said, putting his tools away.

Gabbey shook her head. "No, not at all. Positive comments only."

"Good."

"Did you get your breakfast yet?" Gabbey asked.

"No."

"Better hurry," Gabbey said. "They'll be breaking it down soon. But if you do miss out, sneak back into the kitchen. I'll fix you a plate."

"Okay, thanks."

"No, thank you," Gabbey said. Thinking to herself, *I wonder just how good he is?*

CHAPTER 6

When he finished with the piano, Jason made his way to the breakfast buffet where he made a plate and took it out to the front patio. He didn't realize how far up the hill the cottage sat until he looked at the town of Baddeck below. A large body of water could be seen in the distance. A small lighthouse sat to the left with sailboats attached to moorings close to shore. The far shore was tree-lined, continuing up the side of a mountain. The sun was now over the treetops, and the sky was clear. While there weren't a lot of colors in the scene, it was really quite beautiful.

His stomach growling, Jason turned his attention to his breakfast. This morning he allowed himself sausage, scrambled eggs, and a couple small pastries. He told himself he'd work it off later.

His thoughts turned to what he had to do today. The day was his to organize as he wished. It was the first time in years his life wasn't blocked out in sixty-minute segments. The question: did he have the discipline *not* to live on such a tight clock?

He took a deep breath.

Was that part of the problem, he wondered? He always had something to do, somewhere to be. Class, practice time, study time, lessons, the gym, a run in the park. It was a never-ending cycle, all focused on his music. But at what price?

Were the concerns of Professor Cunningham and his sister justified?

He decided not to do a detailed schedule but simply list what he wanted to accomplish on any particular day.

A gust of wind crossed the patio, causing several strands of hair to fall across his face. Pushing them back in place, he refocused out across the water in the distance.

He smiled as he said softly, "I'll let the wind decide."

His thoughts were interrupted by the sound of barking. Jason looked to his right as two dogs came running across the patio. One was black and large, the other light brown and small. The smaller one was chasing the larger one. They seemed to be having a good time as they circled the area. The chase continued until they came close to Jason's table. Then they came to an abrupt stop, side by side, panting with their tongues out.

Before he could respond, a girl about Jason's age came jogging up. She ignored Jason at first as she pointed a finger at the dogs. "Bear! Louie! What are you two doing? You know better than to be up here bothering the guests." The dogs looked at her, then back at Jason.

"They didn't cause any trouble. They were just having fun," Jason defended. He gave the dogs a wink.

The girl looked at him. Her arm dropped. "Part of the blame is mine," she said. "I didn't realize anyone was out here."

"Again, no harm done. I was just finishing up, anyway."

The girl focused back on the animals and raised her arm. "Go!" she commanded.

The dogs looked at Jason. He swore they gave him a wink

back as they took off down the steps where they turned and headed around the building.

“They really are well trained,” the girl said. “Except when they first wake up. Then their pent-up energy over-rides their training.” She watched until they disappeared. Focusing back on Jason, she said, “Looks like you enjoyed your breakfast. Anything I can get you?”

She was near his height, thin, with an athletic build. Her face was oblong, her complexion clear. Her black hair was braided and hung down her back. She gave off a warm smile. At first Jason thought she was already tanned, then he realized it was her heritage. She wore a red polo shirt with the Baddeck Cottage logo and khaki shorts which showed off her well-developed legs. Her name tag read Noel. All in all, she was amazingly beautiful.

“No thanks, I’m just finishing up...Noel, right?” Jason replied.

Her smile widened as she glanced at her name tag. “Not fair. You don’t have a name tag.”

“Jason...Jason Kinde.” He held out his hand.

She took it without hesitation and with a firm grip. “Noel Summers. Nice to meet you.”

Jason tipped his head slightly to the side. “Summers... Any relation to Gabbey, the owner?”

“Gabbey’s my aunt. Her husband and my father were brothers.” Noel explained, taking a more relaxed posture. “My uncle and father were Mi’kmaq. My mother is as well. We’re First Nations people of Canada’s Atlantic Provinces.”

Jason paused before continuing. “I was born and raised in New York...the city. The population is about as diverse as you can get. Yet, I've never met a genuine North American Indian." Before Noel could respond, he held up his hand. "I think it's kind of cool." Lowering his hand, he continued. "Besides that, you're...you're beautiful." He added quickly, "My mother and sister are both in the fashion industry. I've been around beautiful women all my life."

"Thank you."

"One question though," Jason said. "I thought this area was heavily French. I haven't heard any French spoken since I've been here." It was one piece of information Jason did know before his visit to the area as his sister explained he had better learn French quickly.

Noel smiled as she spouted off a couple sentences in fluent French.

Jason's eyes widened. "I asked for that, didn't I."

More French followed.

"Any other languages?"

Noel converted to English. "English, French and a little of my native tongue, although there are dozens of diverse dialects."

Jason hesitated. "What did you say to me in French?"

She translated, *"Tourists, tourists, tourists... We want their money but sometimes they can be a nuisance."*

"The second thing you said?"

Noel again translated. *"You're not bad-looking yourself."* They both laughed.

Jason took the napkin from his lap, wiped his mouth, and set it on the table. Rising to his feet, he pointed to her uniform shirt. "So, what do you do here, besides chase dogs around?"

Noel smiled. "My title is assistant *to* the manager. When I came here for my interview, I asked Gabbey about my job description. She took a pen and wrote in large letters on a notepad: WHATEVER. I actually have that framed and hanging in my office." She started to clear the dishes away. "I do whatever is needed. It's a good way to learn the business. Gabbey is grooming me to take over when she retires."

"Are you in school?" Jason asked.

"One of the desk clerks and I are taking hotel management online."

"Cindy?"

"Yes. You met her?"

Jason smiled. "You can't miss her when you walk in the front door."

Noel laughed. "She's new and is a little bubbly, but she's a hard worker and is learning fast...just like me."

"Well, she and everyone else have been nice so far."

"Thank you," Noel said. "So, what do you do?"

"I'm in school, too, finishing up my masters," Jason answered.

"A masters in?" Noel coaxed.

Jason hesitated. "Music."

"Cool. What do you play?"

"The piano."

"We have a piano somewhere. I think it's in one of the banquet rooms."

"Actually, it's in the lounge now. Gabbey had it moved so I can practice while I'm here."

"How long are you staying?" Noel asked.

"Scheduled for the whole summer," Jason answered.

"Oh," Noel said surprised. "That's nice. Maybe you can play for us sometime."

"Maybe."

"You here with your family?" Noel continued to query.

"No. I'm alone. Came here for the summer to find some peace and quiet."

Noel waited for additional explanation. When none came, she said, "You found the right place." She finished gathering up the dishes. "Anyway, enjoy your day. I'll see you around."

"I'd like that," Jason said.

Noel gave him a smile as she walked away.

. . . . .

Jason moved to the patio rail. He took a couple deep breaths, enjoying the coolness and freshness of the air.

"Wouldn't get this at home," he muttered softly. He slowly scanned the view before him, absorbing the serenity of the scene. While the view of Central Park from his apartment at home was impressive, this view was....

He paused, trying to come up with an appropriate descriptive. Finally, he decided on *relaxing.* "Relaxing and peaceful," he mouthed. He closed his eyes and worked a kink out of his neck, reviewing the task list he'd made earlier. There was no time schedule attached.

The first task was to check out the piano more thoroughly. He had tuned it to where he wanted and fixed the sticking keys, but he hadn't really given it a workout.

He moved from the railing and headed toward the patio doors. His movement, however, was interrupted by the barking and stampeding of the two dogs from earlier. Seeing him, they came his way, stopping directly in his path. As before, they went to a sitting position, both looking at Jason with friendly eyes.

"Bear and Louie, right?" Jason said with a laugh. The dogs barked on cue. He reached down and gave each a rub on the head. "I don't have any food, sorry." They circled him a couple times before jumping off the patio, looking as if asking him to come and play. Jason shook his head side to side as he said, "So much for checking out the piano."

He started after them, causing the two animals to take off across the lawn.

. . . . .

Noel came out on the patio twenty minutes later looking for the dogs, hoping they weren't bothering any of the guests. Most people didn't mind the animals, but there was always someone who'd comment about them not being leashed. Nole would always apologize, make some excuse, and then give the person one of her best smiles. That usually did the trick. That certainly worked with the guy eating breakfast this morning...Jason. The dogs had immediately taken to him and vice versa. She smiled and thought that it didn't hurt that he seemed nice. He was also quite attractive.

Noel cut the thought off, reminding herself he was a guest.

She made her way out to the patio, whistling for the

dogs. When she didn't get a response, she walked over to the rail and looked out across the yard. To her surprise, the two dogs were out in the middle of the yard with Jason. She could see the trio had been playing. There was a tennis ball lying off to the side. Jason was rubbing Bear across his back. Louie was scampering around trying to get some attention as well.

Taking in the scene, Noel whistled again. This time the two dogs responded and started running in her direction. Jason looked toward her and gave a wave. He rose to his feet and followed the dogs.

The dogs ran up onto the patio and started circling Noel, yipping for attention, which she gladly gave. Jason made it up onto the patio a moment later.

"Sorry," he said. "Didn't mean to take your dogs away from you. We've been running around and playing. I wanted to go for a run anyway."

"No problem. I hope they weren't bothering you."

"Not at all. We had a good time. They gave me a good workout." Jason handed her the tennis ball. "They certainly like to play fetch, although we played more chase than anything."

Noel continued petting the animals. After a moment's hesitation, she said, "So, what do you have planned for the day?"

"I'm going to take a shower and then unpack. I haven't done that yet. Then I want to check out the piano." It was Jason's turn to hesitate. "What's on your agenda?"

"I have to check Gabbey's *whatever* list as she calls it. Although, she told me earlier the local tour I was supposed to take a family on was canceled. One of the kids evidently is sick."

"Local tour?" Jason questioned.

Noel gave the dogs a couple more pets before shooing them away. They didn't hesitate as they took off down the steps and headed across the yard. "This maritime area of Canada is very popular for bus tours," Noel explained. "They're anywhere from three to ten days. They run mostly during the summer and early fall, but we get an occasional spring tour. A large part of our business depends on this. However, we do get families who come here on their own. We offer local excursions to the various attractions in the area. We limit them to day trips only. Either Alex or I usually do these. As long as there are eight people or less, we're okay from the licensing point of view."

"Are there that many things around here to see?" Jason asked.

Noel tipped her head to the side. "You obviously didn't do any homework for this trip, did you?"

Jason gave a shrug. "I want to be surprised."

Noel thought that quite adventurous. "What do you think so far?"

Jason looked out across the patio towards the town and across the lake. The lighthouse sitting near the far shore appeared much clearer today. He turned toward Noel.

"Quiet and peaceful." He gave Noel a wink. "Also, very beautiful."

Noel gave him a chuckle in return. "You should go unpack."

CHAPTER 7

It was mid-afternoon before Jason made it to the lounge area and the piano. Bobby was behind the bar prepping for the day, cutting fruit, filing the beer cooler, and wiping down all the surfaces.

"Do you mind?" Jason said, pointing to the piano.

"Be my guest," Bobby said, straightening up. "I like music." As an afterthought, "What kind of music do you play?"

"I'm training as a classical pianist, but I can play most any kind of music if I have it in front of me."

Bobby motioned toward the piano. "Then let's hear what you've got."

Jason pushed the cover off the keys and started to lift the lid but decided against that. He wasn't sure about the acoustics in the area and how loud it would sound. He sat down, adjusted the seat, and started doing some warm-up exercises. He focused on the tone of the instrument and was quite pleased. He was also satisfied it was tuned to his liking. The previously-sticking keys worked as well. He set his iPad on the music holder and scrolled through to make a selection. Decision made, he adjusted his seat and began to play.

The sound of Beethoven's Piano Concerto #1 filled the air.

Some historians thought this concerto was the first Beethoven piece performed publicly. It was certainly the first classical composition Jason had learned start-to-finish, and his first recital piece at Barret's with a full orchestra. He remembered how strangely confident he'd felt during the recital. The next day, Professor Cunningham congratulated him on his performance, and on getting through the piece with minimal frowns from the conductor, Professor Jamison Heinrich, who served as the music director of the school's orchestra and taught conducting. He was very strict with how a piece of music was interpreted. He was fond of saying "When you play in my orchestra, you will play the music as it is written."

Today, oblivious to the activity around him, Jason played through the concerto, skipping the the orchestra-only sections. Twenty minutes later, he reached the finale and struck the keys with vigor, his fingers moving across the keyboard in a blur. When the final passage was struck, he almost came off the seat. As was his norm at the end of a piece, he sat for a moment with his head bowed.

The silence was broken by an outbreak of applause. Jason turned and looked to the side. There were several people standing at the bar watching him. He had evidently drawn an unintentional audience. He was used to receiving such a reception at his performances, but not during practice time. He quickly regained his composure, rose to his feet where he acknowledged and thanked the people.

Someone yelled out, "encore," which made him laugh.

"I'm just practicing," he explained.

"Well, practice some more," the person commanded in a friendly manner. Others chimed in as well.

Jason saw Gabbey and Noel standing off to the side. Both were smiling and had been applauding with the rest. He gave Gabbey a palms-up shrug as if asking what he should do. She lifted her hands, wiggling her fingers, indicating he should continue. He refocused on the crowd as he placed his hand over his heart to show his appreciation.

Someone in the back called out, "Do you take requests?"

Jason laughed some more. "What do you have in mind?"

"Maybe something you'd play at a piano bar...old standards, show tunes, things like that," the man said.

"Broadway okay?" Jason queried.

"That would be great."

While Barrett Conservatory focused on classical music, after hours one might hear a variety of genres. With the New York school being within walking distance of all the major theaters, Broadway musicals were favorites of many students, Jason included. Jason started playing songs from a variety of popular shows. He played for another twenty minutes. When he finished, there were more people and louder applause. He went right into a medley of old standards his mother and father liked. He looked up and saw people dancing. He broke into a wide smile. It was the first time anyone had ever danced while he played.

When he finished, there was more applause. He stood and again acknowledged the crowd. "How about I get back to practicing and play a couple classical pieces?" No one in the crowd complained.

Later, when Jason announced he was taking a break, the crowd dispersed. Gabbey and Noel came up to him. Gabbey had some Canadian money in her hand. Handing it to Jason, she said, "Next time, put out a tip jar."

Jason stared at the money. "I've never been paid to play before. Plus, this was just practice."

Gabbey motioned for him to take the bills. "Several customers gave me this for you."

Jason started to refuse the money but realized many of the staff at the resort worked for tips. He didn't want to seem unappreciative. He took the money and put it in his pocket.

"Thank you," he said, still bewildered at being paid to play. He picked the cover up off the floor. "I think I'll leave the cover off if you don't mind. Let it continue to breath."

"Fine with me," Gabbey said, taking it from him. "I'll keep it in a closet somewhere. Besides, the piano looks nice sitting there."

Jason nodded. "I'll play some later if it's okay with you?"

"You can play anytime you want," the owner said. "Just remember to put out a tip jar."

Jason laughed. "Whatever."

CHAPTER 8

Jason awoke the next morning refreshed and energized. He couldn't remember ever feeling so rested. He stretched to get a spasm out of his back. He pulled out his iPad to look at his schedule before remembering he had no schedule. He typed a few things he wanted to accomplish but added no specific time marks. He glanced at the clock: 6:00 am. Remembering he wanted to check out the gym, he dressed in workout clothes and headed downstairs.

He walked through the front door of the building and was making his way along the pool when he noticed someone in the water swimming laps. Realizing it was the girl with the dogs, Noel, he paused to watch. Her movement through the water was fluid and quiet. As she touched the wall and turned, he saw she was wearing a one-piece, dark blue, tight-fitting swimsuit. She headed toward the other end of the pool. At the far end she turned again. As she was taking a breath, she noticed him standing on the side. She stopped mid-stroke. Treading water, she pushed her goggles atop of her head.

"Jason! How long have you been standing there?" she demanded, wiping water from her eyes.

"I just walked in. I was on my way to the exercise room," Jason said quickly.

Noel tipped her head to the side as she decided whether to believe him or not. Deciding to give him the benefit of the doubt, she said, "Go ahead in, if you want. I'm almost finished here. I'll check on you in case you have any questions about the equipment."

He started to tell her he had been in a gym before. Instead, "That would be much appreciated."

In the exercise room, he surveyed the equipment. It looked like a pretty standard set-up with nothing he hadn't seen before. He did a few stretching exercises and then started on the machines. He had a personal trainer back home who put him through a routine. He followed this as closely as he could remember. He was halfway through when he heard Noel come through the door. He stopped and rose to his feet as she walked up to him. She was wearing a plain white sundress that clung to her damp bathing suit. Her wet hair hung down her back freely. She looked beautiful. He smiled and said, "Do you swim often?"

She returned the smile. "Every day, when I can. It really depends on how busy we are in the morning. When it gets warmer, I like to swim in the lake."

Jason's eyebrows rose. "Is that safe?"

"Been doing it my whole life," Noel answered. "I only use the pool when the lake water is too cold."

"You looked like you were enjoying it," Jason said.

"I was on the swim team in high school," Noel said. "We never did very well in competition, but we always had a lot of fun. It's a good way to stay in shape."

"Do you use the gym?" Jason asked.

"I like to use the treadmill to cool down. Some days I work out on the weights."

"I was just about to get on the treadmill, if you want to join me," Jason said.

As they ran side by side, Jason said, "Do you ever run outside?"

"That's my evening routine. I love to run along the lakefront as the sun is setting. I find it soothing for my soul," Noel said.

"Maybe I could join you sometime," Jason ventured. "It could be a good way for you to show me the town."

Noel hesitated. "We could do that, I guess."

They continued on the treadmill in silence a few minutes before Noel said, "What do you have planned for your time here?"

"No set schedule. The priority is to get ready for my recital in the fall. I also have a couple papers to do, but that shouldn't be a problem," Jason said. "Other than that, I want to stay in shape and see the area." A few steps later, he added, "I am supposed to meet an Uncle Andy who's going to..." Jason paused in his speech. "I'm not sure what's he going to do...keep an eye on me, I guess. I understand he travels a lot and is out of town at the moment."

"That he does," Noel acknowledged.

"You know him?"

"He's an uncle by a couple marriages down the family tree," Noel explained. "He and his wife had a vacation home here, but when she died from cancer a few years back, he moved here permanently. Again though, he does travel a lot."

"Do you know where he lives?"

"Yes. When you're ready, let me know. I'll take you there."

"That would be nice. Thanks."

"I can show you some of the sites if you have time," Noel said. "If there's room in the van when I take a group, you can tag along." Noel let out a chuckle. "I'm not sure you're going to have a lot of time, though. Our guests may keep you busy playing for them."

Jason responded in a serious tone. "That's fine, but I have to stay focused on getting ready for the recital."

"I'm sure they'll understand," Noel said. "I'm also sure they would be just as happy listening to you practice."

This time Jason's tone was lighter. "Tips may not be as good, however."

Noel laughed. "I'm sure Gabbey will take care of you as long as people stay there eating and drinking."

"I'm not looking for that. I was joking," Jason said defensively.

"I know…I know," Noel responded quickly. "But it's a bonus, so take advantage of it."

Jason didn't tell her that, fortunately, making money had never been a motivator for him. Although, the tips from the day before did make him feel good. It also made Bobby and the other wait staff happy as Jason gave them the tip money from yesterday's morning and evening sessions.

. . . . .

Workout complete, Noel went in to check with her aunt to get her Whatever list. Jason went up to his room to shower and dress for the day. He wasn't a big breakfast person, usually in a hurry to get to class or practice time, but this morning, he was hungry and wanted to eat. As he went down the steps, he cautioned himself about maintaining his diet. He knew that being in a different environment, it would be easy to lose control.

The dining room was crowded with tourists who had arrived the previous afternoon. Jason decided to wait before taking his turn in line. He settled for a cup of coffee and went out to the patio to enjoy the morning sky. He had just sat down when he heard barking in the distance. A moment later, Bear and Louis came up to him. He gave them each a pet before they tore off down the steps, across the yard.

"Oh, to be so carefree," Jason mouthed quietly. They seemed so happy and content. Jason wondered if he would ever be like that.

Sipping his coffee, his mind focused on what he wanted to do on this day. Practicing was next on the list after breakfast. He also wanted to find out something about this Uncle Andy who he was supposed to meet. Jason just hoped he wasn't a counselor. He had always kept his personnel life private. After all, with his music, there was little time for anything else.

A voice behind him broke his train of thought. He looked over his shoulder and saw Noel. "Good morning…again," she said, giving him a wide smile. She was now dressed in a blue polo shirt with khaki shorts, tennis shoes, and white socks. Once again, her hair was braided and hung far down her back.

Jason stared for a moment, soaking in her beauty. "That was fast, the change that is," he said.

She laughed softly. She glanced down at his coffee. "You have breakfast yet?"

"I was waiting for the line to go down," he answered.

"I just came through the dining room. It looks pretty good right now. Want me to fix you a plate?"

"Join me?"

"Thanks, but I'm working now. Gabbey has me covering for her while she runs a few errands."

"I can fix my own," Jason said.

"I really don't mind," Noel insisted.

Minutes later she returned with a freshly made waffle with blueberries, scrambled eggs, and sausage. Setting it in front of him and giving him a set of silverware wrapped in a linen napkin, she said, "If you have any complaints, see the management."

Jason laughed. "I thought you were the management?"

Noel laughed with him. "You got me there."

Jason unrolled the silverware and put the napkin in his lap. "I'm sure I won't have any complaints. And thank you."

"Let me know if you need anything else."

Jason nodded and turned his attention to his food. Letting out a soft chuckle, he figured he better eat before the dogs returned.

. . . . .

When he finished eating, he went into the lounge area. The earlier crowd had cleared out. There were a few people lingering, however. Out of courtesy, Jason asked if anyone minded if he practiced. No one said anything negative. He sat at the piano and started warming up. He set his iPad on the music stand and flipped to the list of pieces he had to prepare for his recital. Most had already been memorized, however, he kept the iPad handy for the rest. The recital was to be approximately forty-five minutes plus an encore. He was preparing over ninety minutes of material, the final decision of what to play to be determined later. He and Dr. Cunningham had decided on a variety of composers – Beethoven, Chopin, Tchaikovsky, and possibly a couple short pieces by Bach. While many pianists he met at competitions had already started focusing on one or two specific composers, he had yet to do that. Dr. Cunningham advised him to stay as broad as possible so that his window of opportunity of where to play and with whom would be more expansive. Besides, Jason found that he liked playing a variety of composers. He also enjoyed wandering outside the realm of classical music, as the crowd the night before had enjoyed.

Today, he focused on pieces for the recital. The guests in the dining room seemed content with this. Several stopped by to tell him they enjoyed his playing. When he was finished two and a half hours later, he found several Canadian coins lying atop the piano. He put the money aside to give to Bobby later for distribution among the staff.

Overall, it was a good session, and Jason was pleased with his playing. He closed the cover over the keys and went to find Gabbey to ask about the man he was supposed to meet. As he headed across the lobby, Noel came from the opposite direction.

She said, "Jason, I was just coming to look for you."

Jason threw his hands into the air. "I swear I didn't complain about breakfast."

Noel laughed. "I came to tell you that Uncle Andy called and said he should be here sometime late this afternoon or early evening. He's fogged in in Halifax."

"Okay, thanks," Jason said. He started to walk away, his curiosity about this Uncle Andy continuing to rise.

He stopped when Noel spoke. "What are you doing the rest of the day?" she said.

"I don't have anything specific planned. I was going to take a break and practice more later." Jason responded. "Why, what did you have in mind?"

"Just asking," she said. "I have to go down to the grocery store in town. It's right on the waterfront. The owner called Gabbey this morning to let her know they got a delivery of fresh fruit and vegetables. I don't know where they got them this time of year, but I'm going to check it out. I thought you might like to tag along, eh? I can show you the town, including where Uncle Andy lives."

Jason glanced at his watch. "When are you going?"

"I'm ready now."

"Then lead the way."

As they headed toward the van, Jason asked, "Why doesn't whoever delivers to the grocery store bring a delivery up here? It would save you all time and money."

"You're right, we would save some money," Noel replied, "but the store is owned by a third-generation elderly couple who have been there for years. Everyone in the community depends on the store. So, we support it whenever we can. Plus, somewhere along the line, they're family."

"Sounds like everybody around here is related in one way

or another," Jason commented. Besides his parents and his sister, he didn't have much contact with family. His aunts and uncles all lived in different parts of the United States.

"That they are," Noel agreed. As they got to the van, she let out a loud whistle that startled Jason. "Sorry," she said opening the side door.

Jason heard the two dogs scampering around the corner at full speed. He thought they were going to run into Noel before sliding to a halt right at her feet. She reached down and gave them each a pet.

"Want to go to Aunt Judy's and get some treats?" she said, motioning them into the van. They didn't have to be asked twice as they ran over each other trying to be the first one in.

It was a beautiful clear morning with only a slight breeze blowing east to west. The early morning had been a bit chilly, but as the sun rose over the mountains, the air quickly warmed. Jason turned and glanced toward Noel. He wondered why he was so attracted to her. Why was he having such strong feelings, and so quickly, no less? He had been around a lot of beautiful women in his life. There had even been a few short-term relationships. He'd always argued he didn't have time and definitely didn't want to make any sort of commitment. Now, he had time. He tried arguing that she was just part of the entire aura he was experiencing. He turned and faced forward.

. . . . .

Noel took the scenic route down to the waterfront. She weaved through the streets, pointing out various historical sites along the way. Uncle Andy's house was included in the tour. The town and surrounding areas were weathered but well maintained. When they got to the waterfront, they slowly drove along the main street. Noel pointed out several bars and restaurants, tourist attractions and stores. They pulled into a parking lot directly on the waterfront. To their left was a one-story, metal, fabricated building that Noel said was the grocery store. Next to that was a pier that extended a couple hundred feet out onto the lake. At the beginning of the pier was a restaurant. There were several tables of people sitting outside enjoying the weather. Noel explained that the end of the dock was where her Uncle Henry docked his tour boat. He'd be bringing it from winter storage soon.

"Uncle Henry?" Jason said with a grin.

"Yes," Noel said without further explanation.

She turned off the van and went around to open the sliding doors. Bear and Louie were out as soon as they could fit through the opening. They barked a couple times as they scampered toward the grocery store.

"No leashes?" Jason commented.

"Everyone in town knows them," Noel said.

"What about tourists?"

Noel laughed. "Bear and Louie are the town's ambassadors. If you don't know them now, you will in a few minutes."

"Another difference between here and back home," Jason said. "New York has strict leash laws."

"Whatever works for your community, I guess," Noel

said. "There are advantages for living in a rural community," she added.

Jason made no comment as he followed her toward the warehouse-looking building. The country was not turning out to be quite what Jason had expected. Nor were the people.

Most of the waterfront-side of the store consisted of sliding glass doors now open to let in the comfortable breeze off the lake. There were a couple of people going in with empty bags. Several people came out with their bags full. Calling them by name, Noel said hello to each.

The inside was brightly lit by overhead fluorescent lights. The floor was smooth concrete. There were old-fashioned grocery carts available as you entered. Jason couldn't help but notice how different the shopping experience was from the city. No one was in a hurry. Everyone was patient. Conversations between customers and staff were abundant. The store was laid out in a typical parallel aisle fashion, except there was no rhyme or reason as to how the merchandise was displayed on the shelves.

Noel grabbed a shopping cart and headed for the first aisle. "If you see something you want, toss it in," she added.

Jason stayed close to her. "People in New York would go crazy in a place like this, not finding what they wanted and not getting out quickly," he said.

They continued shopping in silence with Jason dropping in some protein bars as well as a bag of rice cakes. At the end of the third aisle, they came to a display of fruits and vegetables that were still in their delivery crates with a sign announcing they had just arrived.

"This is what we came for," Noel said.

As they started to bag up tomatoes, an elderly lady came up to them. She was tall. thin, and wore her hair in a bun. Glasses sat in front of the bun atop her head. She was dressed in coveralls with rubber boots on her feet.

"Hey, sweetheart, I see you got my message."

Noel held out her arms and gave the lady a hug. "We did. Thanks so much for the heads up. You know how much Cookie likes to work with fresh produce."

"Well, if there's anything else you need or we can do for you, let us know," the woman said. "And tell Cookie that the last batch of soup he sent down the other day was delicious ...and thanks so much."

"Will do," Noel said. She turned toward Jason. "By the way, this is Jason Kinde. Jason, this is Aunt Judy."

"The famous Aunt Judy," Jason said, accepting the outstretched hand. The woman's grip was firm, her hands calloused.

"It's a pleasure to meet you, Jason," the woman said. She glanced at Noel. "Boyfriend?"

Noel shook her head and replied quickly. "No. He's a guest at the cottage. I'm just showing him around."

The elder woman gave the younger woman a skeptical look. Looking back at Jason, she continued. "Welcome to Baddeck, Mr. Jason. I hope you enjoy your stay."

"I have so far," Jason said.

"He's a pianist," Noel said. "You ought to hear him. He's quite good."

"You ought to introduce him to Uncle Andy," the woman said.

"We'll have to do that," Noel said, giving Jason a wink.

"I'll let you get back to your shopping," Aunt Judy said. "When you get checked out, I'll have someone help you load up."

"Thanks," Noel said as the woman started walking away. After a couple steps, the grocer turned and looked over her shoulder. "A guest my foot," she spouted.

They finished shopping, which included several cases of fresh fruits and vegetables. As promised, Aunt Judy had a couple of her staff help load the van. She came out as the last cart was emptied. Louie and Bear were at her side, each looking satisfied with their visit so far. Aunt Judy shook hands with Jason, telling him to make sure he came back soon. She gave Noel a hug and told her to do the same. As they broke apart, Noel reached into her pocket and pulled out some folded Canadian bills. She peeled off a couple and stuffed them into Aunt Judy's pocket. "You take this and go out to eat tonight with your husband," she directed.

"You don't have to do that," Aunt Judy protested.

"You're right, I don't. But I did. Now do as I say."

This earned her another hug. "You know you're the sweetest girl around here?" Aunt Judy said, making eye contact with Jason.

"I'm only sweet because of inheriting the sugar from you," Noel countered. Closing the van's rear doors, she added, "Mind if I leave the van here a few minutes while I show Jason the pier?"

"Take him to lunch. They're open."

"I would except Cookie is waiting for me. You know how anxious he can get."

"You tell Cookie I said to hold onto his britches. If not, I'm going to come up there and glue 'em up, eh," Aunt Judy threatened.

"I will," Noel promised with a laugh. She grabbed Jason's arm. "Come on, let's go take a look around." She turned her attention to the two dogs. "Lead the way, you guys."

The two dogs turned and headed across the parking lot.

Bear and Louie went ahead of them, smelling and looking for anything of interest. They turned and headed toward the wide industrial sized pier. There were several commercial fishing boats tied along the left side. A couple small runabouts were mixed in. Jason looked out and saw a series of sailboats attached to mooring buoys. They looked so calm and so peaceful floating on the serene water. Against the opposite shore, he saw the lighthouse he had noticed before. At first, he thought it was out of place as there didn't seem to be a need for such a structure, but he didn't know the size or the depth of the lake. Plus, the more he stared at it, the more he realized it gave one's eyes a point of focus. It was picturesque, if nothing else.

They walked toward a two-story rectangular building which housed the restaurant. The building was made of wood with slated shingles. There was a patio deck surrounding three sides of the first floor. The building looked weathered but well maintained.

"The name of the place is Box On The Dock," Noel explained. "It may not look like much, but it has great food, mostly from area farms and suppliers. It's also one of the hangouts for both locals and tourists in the summer."

"Interesting name," Jason said. "Kind of a play on words."

"Exactly," Noel agreed. "Two doctors – husband and wife – sold their practice several years ago and bought the place. It was pretty rundown, but they turned it around. They have one of the best chefs, too. He's actually the son of one of the tour bus drivers who comes to the cottage frequently."

Jason couldn't resist the next thought that crossed his mind. "Not a cousin?"

"No," Noel laughed. "They're from Prince Edward Island."

She led Jason around to the waterside of the building. They found Thomas, the cook, washing out some big pots. He was a short, stocky man about Jason's age. He wore a white chef's top and black pants. His head was covered in a cap with the restaurant's name across the front. Noticing them, he looked up and turned off the water.

"Noel, what brings you to town this time of day?"

Noel started to give him a hug but stopped when she saw how wet he was. She laughed. "I owe you a hug," she said. She pointed at Jason. "This is Jason Kinde. He's staying at the cottage for the summer. I'm showing him around. We were at Aunt Judy's picking up some produce, and I thought we'd come over and say hello."

"She texted me earlier and said she got a load of fresh produce in," the chef said. "I hope you saved me some."

"She had plenty when I left a couple minutes ago," Noel said. "But if you want to run over there really quick, I'm going to take Jason out to the end of the pier and show him around. I can always give you some of what we have if there's a problem."

"I know where you live if needed."

"Remember, you have to get past Cookie first."

"He can cook, but he can't bake worth a damn," Thomas said with a humorous grunt. "I made a couple cheesecakes early this morning. That'll serve as bait if need be."

"Thomas makes the best cheesecake around," Noel explained to Jason.

"Go ahead and finish showing Jason around," Thomas said. "Stop back when you're done. I'll brew a fresh pot of coffee, and you can tell me if the cheesecake meets your standards." Looking at Jason, he added "Noel here is one of my taste testers. One thing I like…or don't like…about her is that she's truthful to the core."

"Tells it like it is, eh," Jason said.

Thomas tipped his head to the side. "How long have you been here, Jason?"

"Couple days, why?" Jason answered with a perplexed expression.

"You've already picked up the dialect, *eh.*"

Jason looked to Noel for help. She gave him a wide smile as she took him by the arm. "I'll explain as we walk."

Thomas laughed. "You guys go ahead. I'll finish up here, then I'll run next door to make sure Aunt Judy saves me something."

"Remember, she likes your cheesecake, too." Noel quipped.

As they headed toward the end of the pier, Jason said, "Thomas's cheesecakes must be good if they are so popular."

"They are that," Noel said. "Plus, if anyone needs any

kind of a donation for any fundraiser in town, Thomas is always there with a cheesecake or two."

"It's good that he supports the community," Jason said.

"Everyone supports the community around here."

Jason stopped and turned toward Noel. "Not only does everyone support the community, everyone supports each other. One restaurant willing to give up fresh produce and vegetables to a competitor is not just family, it's something ingrained into the people of this town."

"Yes," Noel said. "But I don't think it's specific to Baddeck. Small communities have different needs than larger ones." She paused, putting her arm through Jason's. "Let me ask you this. When you walk round where you live, how many people do you see that you know? How many people do you see that you can actually stop and talk to?"

Jason paused. "I get your point." He looked around at the people in the area. He glanced out at the water and then looked back at the town. He hadn't known what to expect when he first came to Baddeck, but it certainly wasn't what he was experiencing.

Noel tightened her grip on his arm. "Let's finish the tour so we can get back and have a piece of cheesecake."

They walked a few steps arm in arm before Noel put his arm down but stayed close to him. Jason could smell the scent of her shampoo. It felt good to be close to her. He wondered if she felt the same.

They stopped at the end of the pier and took in the view. The lighthouse, not all that tall, continued to draw Jason's eyes to it. The boats sat at their moorings motionless. The sun continued to shine brightly, and the water remained calm. There was an occasional breeze, but overall, the weather was perfect for the time of year.

Noel pointed to the right. "This is the area where the one of the tour boats, *My First Lady III*, docks. She goes out several times a day in season. Captain Henry, who is also a relative, is a third-generation captain of these boats. He has a couple small sailboats he can take people out on if they want the experience of sailing. It's a beautiful body of water to explore. It's actually a large estuary called the Bras d'Or Lake. Some call it Lake Baddeck. It's connected to the North Atlantic, so it's tidal and salt water but also has a lot of influx of freshwater from the connecting rivers.

"The town of Baddeck is at the beginning, and the end, of the Cabot Trail. The Cabot Trail is basically a road that winds its way through Cape Breton. It's about three hundred kilometers, some hundred and eighty miles. It's quite beautiful."

"Baddeck sits on the trail?" Jason asked for clarification.

"It's kind of a loop," Noel explained.

Jason pointed to the lighthouse across the way. "Does that have a name?"

"It's called Kidston Island Lighthouse." Her arm moved to the right. "If you see the break in the tree line over there, that's the Bell estates. Alexander Graham Bell came to Baddeck and fell in love with the area. He built those houses which you can see along the shoreline. He also built a laboratory. There's a museum nearby I can take you to if you'd like."

"I'd like that," Jason said. He continued surveying the

scene as he said, "My sister bought me a couple of tourist books. I looked at the pictures. They don't do this area justice."

"I'm glad you're enjoying your stay so far," Noel said. "If there's anything I can do for you, let me know."

Jason wanted to add just how much he was enjoying his visit, but Bear and Louie began showing their impatience to move forward.

Giving his arm a tug, Noel added, "There is one thing you can do for *me*, though."

"What's that?"

"Lead the way back to the cheesecake and coffee."

Turning and facing the shore, Jason pointed in that direction. "Bear…Louie…you guys lead the way."

As if fully understanding the command, the two dogs tore off down the pier.

"I didn't mean quite that quickly," Jason yelled as he took Noel's arm in his.

CHAPTER 9

After cheesecake and coffee, they returned to the cottage where Jason helped Noel unload the van. Cookie was waiting for them. Surveying the produce, he said, "Fish stew for dinner tonight? A friend dropped off a few trout he caught this morning."

Noel looked toward Jason. "How does that sound to you?"

Jason frowned. "Can't say I've ever had fish stew before."

Before Noel could say anything, her phone rang. It was Gabbey telling her that the afternoon tour bus was going to be early. She said goodbye to Cookie and Jason as she headed towards the lobby. Cookie grabbed the piece of cheesecake they'd brought for him and headed for the kitchen. Jason went to the lounge. Bobby hadn't opened the bar yet, but there were a few people sitting around the high-top tables. Jason nodded to a couple of people he recognized and pointed to the piano.

"Mind if I play a bit?"

No one objected.

He played for two hours before going up to his room. He saw housekeeping had been in and noticed a couple potted plants sitting around. He made a mental note to thank Gabbey when he saw her next. He laid across the bed to rest for a few minutes. Unintentionally, a few minutes turned into a couple of hours. The change in light and increased breeze through the window woke him. He sat up with a start. Glancing around, he stretched and yawned. The clock showed he had time for a visit to the gym before dinner. He decided to stay in-house for dinner and try some fish stew. Besides, he wanted to get back to the piano. He was concerned he wasn't practicing enough.

. . . . .

The fish stew was excellent, the mixture of flavors quite unique. The recommended wine pairing was a dry white from a local vineyard. Knowing he was going to practice after dinner, Jason only took a taste. He had always been skeptical about wine pairings, but this one was spot on. The dining room was crowded with tourists and a few locals, so Jason ate at the bar with Bobby. They talked about the fish stew and cheesecake. Bobby reiterated that Thomas's cheesecake was a community favorite.

Jason spent more time at the bar than he intended. He told himself not to get into bad habits; he still had a lot of work to do. He signed his check, left cash for a tip, and headed over to the piano. He recognized several people in the crowd who started clapping before he even sat down. He made a mental note to stay focused, which he did with the compromise of playing an occasional request as the evening went along.

After two hours or so, he ended with a short Beethoven piece. He rose to his feet and thanked everyone for their support. It was then he noticed a bowl filled with money sitting on the piano. He took the bowl and pulled the cover over the keys indicating he was finished for the evening. He told everyone he'd be back at breakfast.

He took a seat at the end of the bar. Bobby was there waiting for him with a glass of wine. Jason set the tip bowl on the bar. "Split this between you and the rest of the staff," he directed.

Bobby slid the bowl beneath the bar as he said. "You know Jason, you don't have to do that every night. You're earning that money just like we earn ours."

"I came here to decompress and practice, not work," Jason said.

"Okay, thank you then," Bobby said. "You do sound great. I hope you're enjoying yourself as well."

"I am so far." Jason picked up his glass of wine and toasted Bobby before taking a long swallow.

"You hungry?" Bobby asked.

Jason let out a laugh. "I could go for some more of Cookie's fish stew."

Bobby returned shortly with a steaming bowl of fish stew. The bartender refilled the wine glass as well. "No charge for the stew. Tradition is that the last serving in the pot is free."

Bobby stepped away and headed toward a few new customers. Jason took a sip of the wine and then began eating the stew. It tasted better than before.

When he finished his meal, Jason slid the empty bowl forward. As he took a sip of wine, an elderly gentleman who had just sat next to him spoke. "You have a phenomenal set of hands, young man."

Jason turned to look at the man, who sported a rather unkempt head of gray hair and wore wire rimmed glasses. He had a bushy mustache. His skin was weathered, his eyes dark. He was stocky and a little overweight. Jason noticed his fingers were long, his nails well kept. In spite of the season, he wore a tweed sports jacket over a white dress shirt without a tie.

Jason tipped his head to the side. There was something familiar about the man. "Thank you. I hope you enjoyed it," he said.

Pointing toward the piano, the man said, "The old girl never sounded so good. I don't know the last time she was even played. I would have thought she'd be out of tune."

"It...she was," Jason said with a shrug.

The man hesitated. "You tuned it?"

Another shrug. "There were a couple sticky keys, too."

"You tune, you repair, and you play. That's a nice repertoire."

Jason said nothing, instead taking another swallow of wine.

"I also like your mix of classical music with standards," the man said.

"I try to please the crowd." Jason said.

"That can be a tough thing to do."

"I really wouldn't know. I'm just a student here practicing for the summer."

"I know," the man said.

Before Jason could respond, Bobby came up to them and said, "Uncle Andy! You're back. We were worried about you."

"Fog was heavy in Halifax, but I got here."

"What are you drinking?"

The man pointed to Jason's glass. "Any of that left?"

Bobby poured a glass of wine and set it in front of him. He also topped off Jason's glass. The older man took a small sip. "You have a good taste in wine too, young man."

"Thank you," Jason said with a smile. "It was the pairing with the fish stew tonight." Jason set his glass down. "Are you the Uncle Andy I'm supposed to be meeting with?"

"Are you Jason Kinde?"

Jason held out his hand. "I am."

The man returned the handshake. "Andrew Summers… Uncle Andy to my friends."

Jason's eyes widened as his recognition of the man kicked in. "Andrew Summers…the…?"

Uncle Andy's finger went up to his mustache-covered lips. He leaned in towards Jason. "Yes, I am. But I like to stay incognito while I'm home."

"Andrew Summers," Jason repeated softly. "It's an honor to meet you, sir. How did you…." The young pianist couldn't think how to finish the question. "And your last name. It's the same as…."

The man looked around to make sure no one could overhear them. "My father was born here, but he moved to Boston when he was young to study music and eventually play in the Boston Pops. He met my mother, who was also in the orchestra. They married and started a family. I'm the third of five children, and the only one who followed our parent's musical pathway. My brothers and sisters are scattered all over the country in different professions. Unfortunately, both of my parents and oldest brother have passed."

"I'm sorry to hear that," Jason said. "What brought you back to Baddeck?" he asked cautiously.

"I moved back here permanently a couple years ago after my wife passed."

Jason was having a hard time believing that he was sitting next to the world-renowned conductor and composer, Andrew Summers. The man had been an associate conductor of the Boston Pops and Boston Symphony for many years, and guest-conducted all over the world. He had won several Oscars for his movie scores and two Tony Awards for his Broadway musicals. There was also a large portfolio of modern-day classical symphonies and other pieces. His work transcended all generations.

Jason wasn't one to get starstruck, but Andrew Summers was someone he'd never dreamed he'd have the opportunity to meet, much less speak with. It made the whole situation surreal. Aloud, "You're retired?"

"Guest-conducting only. That way I control how much I work."

"Wow. . . ." Jason turned his head away when he realized he was staring. "I'm supposed to be meeting with you while I'm here."

"Joseph Cunningham and I have been close friends for many tears," Uncle Andy said. "We talk regularly. When he called a couple months ago, he told me about you. He asked if I would be willing to work with you."

"I didn't know you worked with individual students," Jason said, still star-struck.

"I don't, normally. But if someone asks for a consultation,

so to speak, and I have the time, I'll do it." He emptied his own wine glass. "I told Joseph that I would be spending most of the summer here and if he wanted to send you up, I'd have a listen. He assured me I wouldn't be disappointed. And I haven't been so far."

"Did Dr. Cunningham tell you I'm preparing for my masters recital?" Jason asked.

"He did." The conductor nodded to Bobby as two new glasses of wine were set before them. He took a sip before turning toward Jason. "I want you to come to my home where I can better focus on your playing." He took another swallow of wine. "What are you doing tomorrow morning?"

Jason pointed to the piano. "I plan to be here during breakfast."

"You know where I live?" Uncle Andy asked.

"Noel showed me."

"Then I'll see you after breakfast. Say 9:00 am?"

Jason nodded his agreement.

The conductor took some money out of his wallet and dropped it on the bar. "You should try some of the other wines from this vineyard. They're all very good." He emptied his glass, turned and walked away.

CHAPTER 10

Andrew Summers' house was similar to the other homes along the street. It was a wooden two-story structure, stained a dark brown. There was a wide, covered porch that ran the width of the house. With the house being in the middle of town on a back to front downward slope, it had an excellent view of the waterfront and lake. Inside, there was a large foyer with antiques set about, giving a welcoming atmosphere. The foyer's floor was highly polished hardwood reflecting the morning light streaming in the front window. Uncle Andy met Jason at the front door and escorted him into the music room off to the right.

There were large windows on two sides. This floor was covered in a plush light-brown carpet. Walls were paneled in a similarly colored wood. Lighting was from a series of recessed fixtures. There were many photographs on the walls from Andrew Summer's many years of composing and performing. Mixed in were photos of family and friends, including one of himself and Joseph Cunningham on stage at some unrecognizable concert hall. In the far corner, there were two large curio cabinets containing awards the man had won over the years. However, the bulk of the room was taken up by a white Steinway grand piano.

Jason walked around the room taking a close look at the various photographs. He stopped at the curios. *Such achievements,* he thought. He then turned his attention to the piano. Wanting to say something that didn't sound amateurish, he spoke softly.

"Very nice room. It represents a lifetime of work. Like a visual biography."

"I never heard this room described in that way before," Uncle Andy said. "That's very kind of you."

Jason turned and looked at the man. "It's very kind of you to share this with me."

"My pleasure. Can I offer you something to drink…coffee, tea, water?"

"I'm fine, thank you."

The conductor pointed toward the piano. "I'm going to go get a cup of coffee. You go sit down and get a feel for the girl. When I get back, we'll get started."

The man turned and left the room. Jason sat and adjusted the bench. He closed his eyes and pulled in a couple deep breaths.

Eyes opened, a couple more deep breaths, his hands hovered above the keys. He played a few exercises to get the touch and tone of the instrument. Every piano was different. This one was well tuned with a beautiful tone. Jason quickly realized the room had been set up acoustically. He speculated that the ceiling, which looked like painted overlay, was actually acoustical tiles. The walls were probably designed the same.

He started to play additional exercises when he stopped suddenly. He realized he was sitting at an instrument played by one of the most famous conductors and composers in the world. A streak of fear went through his body. *What if I don't live up to Andrew Summers' expectations,* he thought. It was the first time in a long time he felt nervous, and there was only an audience of one.

Reaching up and touching the music stand, he continued aloud, "I won't let you down, girl, if you won't let me down."

Uncle Andy's voice startled him. "I talk to the piano, too...quite often, I might add."

"Does she listen?" the young pianist asked, glancing over his shoulder.

Uncle Andy let out a puff of air. "Do women ever listen?"

Focusing back on the piano and striking a couple keys, Jason added, "Her tone is beautiful."

"I agree," the composer said. He walked up and put his free hand on the lid, gently tapping his fingers against the wood. "She was originally built for a well-to-do family in Boston. The husband and wife had one daughter, and they wanted her to play the piano. It was the only piano the daughter ever played." Taking a sip of coffee, he looked directly at Jason. "Care to guess the issue?"

Jason hesitated. Previous words from Dr. Cunningham came to mind. Paraphrasing, he said, "It takes several components to become a musician, regardless of the level. First is desire. Second is the discipline to practice. Third is to be in a position where you have the opportunity to practice. Fourth is raw talent. If any one of these components are lacking, well..." Jason shrugged. "I suspect the daughter was lacking several of these components."

Uncle Andy smiled a moment before his expression

turned serious. "The girl lacked the desire and thus the discipline. Her mother naturally blamed it all on the piano. She actually said, and I quote, 'there must be something wrong with the piano if my daughter can't play it.' Already strong patrons, they donated it to the Boston Symphony. I was an associate conductor at the time. We had no use for a white piano, so I bought it way above cost and had it shipped here."

Jason shook his head side to side. "What happened to the daughter, do you know?"

Uncle Andy nodded in the affirmative. "The daughter, who loved to listen to music by the way, came up to me at a fundraiser years later and thanked me for saving her life, as she dubbed it." He laughed. "She's now one of Boston's most sought-after orthopedic surgeons and a strong supporter of the Boston Symphony." He took a seat on one of the chairs and set the coffee cup on a coaster. "Enough talking. Let's hear something you're preparing for the recital."

Jason nodded, turned to face the piano, took a deep breath and started to play.

. . . . .

Jason was sitting at the piano in the cottage's lounge when Noel walked by. She seemed to be in a hurry, but seeing him, she slowed and turned in his direction.

"What's you doing?" she asked, coming up to him.

"Taking a break to look for a couple songs people requested." He pointed to the iPad he was holding.

"That's nice...that you take requests, that is."

Jason shrugged. "Keeps them sitting and drinking. You guys have been very good to me, especially when it comes to using the piano. I figure it's the least I can do in return."

"You don't owe us anything, especially since you give your tips away every night," Noel said. "Anyway, how did your meeting with Uncle Andy go?"

Turning to face her, Jason said, "It was very interesting. His home is quite spectacular, especially the music room. I usually don't get starstruck, but just to be in the same room with the man…last night here at the bar and this morning in his home."

"Uncle Andy is no different than you or me," Noel said.

"Except his curio cabinets have a few more awards than mine."

"I've been in other rooms, and yes, the whole house is wonderful," Noel said.

"Not what I was expecting here in Baddeck."

"That's what makes it even more special," Noel said. "Anyway, what did he think of your playing?"

"He didn't say anything the whole time I played," Jason said. "When I finished, he rose to his feet, looked at his watch and announced we were finished for the day. He said he would see me at the same time, same place tomorrow. He said he'd give me a full assessment after our third day when I took him to lunch."

Noel thought a moment. "I guess he wants to get a more complete picture before he makes any judgment." She smiled. "I do know he likes to go to lunch. I've gone with him several times."

"He seems to like his privacy, though," Jason said.

Noel nodded in agreement. "He does keep a low profile around here. Most locals know who he is and respect his privacy."

Further conversation was stopped by the buzzing of Noel's phone. She listened for a moment. "That's Cindy. There's evidently someone at the front desk who insists they have a reservation, but it's not in the system." Pointing to the piano, she added, "You get back to practicing and I'll get back to work." She turned and walked away.

"I'll see you later?" Jason ventured.

She looked over her shoulder and gave him a smile.

The first notes of a Beethoven piece filled the air.

CHAPTER 11

The next day Jason was again met at the door by Andrew Summers and escorted into the music room. He warmed up while Uncle Andy went for his coffee. During their session, Jason played additional works he was preparing for the recital, telling Uncle Andy that the final program would be decided by himself and Dr. Cunningham.

On the third day, Uncle Andy came into the room with a cell phone and asked permission to record him playing. Jason agreed. When he finished, Uncle Andy rose to his feet and announced it was time for lunch. He said nothing else. They walked to the Box On The Dock restaurant. The hostess, who called the conductor by name, sat them at a table in the corner overlooking the lake.

Uncle Andy introduced Jason to their waitress as a friend from out of town. She also called him by name. The waitress took their beverage order. When she returned with a coffee and iced tea, she told them the lunch special was meatloaf, mashed potatoes, and fresh mixed vegetables. Both ordered the special. Watching the waitress walk away, the young pianist tried to recall the last time he'd had meatloaf, if ever.

Uncle Andy took a swallow of his coffee before setting his cell phone on the table. "Watch this and tell me what you see."

Jason pulled the phone closer and focused on the screen. This image came up of him playing earlier. There was no sound.

"It's muted on purpose," Uncle Andy said.

A confused look crossed Jason's face. "I don't understand."

"I want you to watch, not listen."

Jason looked at the screen as directed. The recording was about three minutes, broken into thirty to forty second segments. When it was finished, Uncle Andy asked, "What did you see?"

Unsure how to answer, Jacob said, "I saw myself playing the piano."

"And?"

Jason sat back, confused. "I'm not sure what you want me to see, sir."

"Fair enough," the conductor said. "How about I tell you what I see?"

Jason nodded.

The maestro began immediately. "I see a young man who is an exceptional pianist who has the four components necessary to succeed that we discussed before: desire, discipline, support and talent. He also plays with an intensity that is rare.

"However, it's this intensity that's bothersome to me. If you look closely, you'll see the veins in your neck bulging. You are also breathing heavily. You are about as far from being relaxed as possible. And that comes through in your playing."

Unable to control his frustration, Jason pointed to the phone and said, "I'm playing in front of one the most famous conductors in the world. How am I to feel anything but intense?"

"Very good point," Uncle Andy said. "I acknowledge the stress one can have performing in front of someone like me.

The desire to please can be overwhelming. However, I observed the same intensity the other night at the cottage. First, I noticed how stiff your neck seemed to be, then I noticed your breathing."

"Where are we headed with this?" Jason said, trying to keep the distress from his voice.

The conductor ignored the question. Instead, "Tell me about yourself, Jason, about your life."

Jason took a breath to relax and a sip of his iced tea. "I was born and raised in Manhattan. I have a twin sister, Laura, who I share an apartment with overlooking Central Park. My parents have the penthouse apartment above us. I was educated at a private school in Manhattan. When I graduated, I was fortunate enough to be accepted at the Barrett Conservatory of Music. I earned my undergraduate degree two years ago. I'm working on my masters in piano performance and plan to be finished by the end of this year, pending a couple papers and the final recital."

"When did you start playing?"

"My parents always had a piano in their apartment as part of the décor. I started playing as soon as I was able to sit on the bench without falling over, at least that's what my mother tells everyone. In reality, I was around four when I started private lessons.

"It was at one of the many cocktail parties that my parents hosted when my mother asked me to play for the guests. There just happened to be someone from Barrett in attendance. The woman heard me, was impressed and asked if I would like to participate in Barret's young musician program.

I was eight at the time. I progressed quickly, and like I said, was accepted to the conservatory full-time when I completed high school. To this day, I feel that cocktail party was a pivotal point in my career."

Uncle Andy smiled. "Did you ever feel pressured by your parents?"

"Never!" Jason said immediately. "I know from other students at school that is a little unusual. Many of my friends claim one of the biggest stressors in their life is parental pressure to succeed."

"I've seen parental pressure ruin more than one career," Uncle Andy said.

"The only thing my father ever told me was that he and my mother would always support my music, but I had to put in the work. I always thought that was a fair trade off," Jason said.

Their waitress brought out generous portions of meatloaf, mashed potatoes, and vegetables. Jason stared at the plate of food.

Uncle Andy said, "Is there a problem?"

"No…No," Jason quickly said. "It's just that I don't think I've ever had meatloaf before."

The conductor took a large bite of meat and said, "If you are successful and travel around the world, you will experience different cultures and cuisines. Keep an open mind, you'll be surprised."

Jason took the advice and started eating. He totally enjoyed his meal. Both declined dessert, but Uncle Andy requested a piece of cheesecake to go.

Settling back in his chair, the conductor said, "Tell me about your parents."

Jason nodded. "My father is a stock analyst on Wall Street. He specializes in overseas markets. Because of the time zones, he works strange hours. My mother is a fashion designer and has a studio in Manhattan. She also has stores in London and Paris. Because of this, she travels a lot."

"And your sister?"

"Laura works for my mother. She's become an exceptional designer herself. The assumption is that she will someday take over the business."

Uncle Andy nodded as he took a sip of coffee. "Tell me about your daily routine."

"During the week, I get up at 6:00 am, eat a light breakfast, and then practice for an hour or so before heading to school. Classes and practice time start at 8:00 am. I'm now working with Dr. Cunningham, so there's two or three hours with him mixed in each week as well. School officially ends at 4:00 pm. Then I go to the gym, usually followed by a run in Central Park. I go home, have dinner around 7:00 pm, practice some more, and do whatever homework I have. On the weekends I catch up on my homework and practice. My parents include my sister and I in their social activities whenever possible, including many charity functions. My parents also entertain a lot at home to which my sister and I are usually invited."

Uncle Andy blew out a huff of air. "No girlfriend? No friends?"

"No time," Jason responded immediately.

"Sounds like you're pretty much focused on your music," Uncle Andy said.

"Is that a problem?" Jason asked defensively.

"It's not for me to say whether it's a problem or not," Uncle Andy replied. "I can tell you this...from experience, mind you...becoming a musician at the caliber you're seeking is a long, arduous journey."

"What do I need to do?" Jason asked solemnly.

Uncle Andy finished his coffee before answering. "In my opinion, you are on a dangerous path, one lacking spontaneity and passion. You're so focused on the journey, you've taken no time to see the beauty of life around you. I'm not saying you don't enjoy what you do, but you lack passion as you do it. As a result, to use one of Professor Cunningham's many analogies, you play like a runaway train. The final destination, your recital at the end of the summer, is now in view. The question: when you finish, where will you be, and what will the cost have been?"

Jason rose to his feet and walked to the open window. There were a few clouds in the sky. The mountain range across the way was brightly lit by the afternoon sun. The lake's surface showed only a few ripples. The top of the lighthouse reflected the sun back at him. A warmth came over him as he focused on the scene. A chill followed as he thought about the maestro's words...a similar theme to Dr. Cunningham's comments.

Just a few weeks ago, Jason thought everything was fine. He was doing well in his classes. His music was progressing the same. Then the confrontation with Dr. Cunningham, followed by the conversation with his sister. Something was wrong, or so they claimed. He was on a dangerous path. So on their advice, he travelled to Baddeck where he met Andrew Summers, whose message was similar.

Staring across the lake, Jason realized for the first time they were right. He was on a dangerous track. It was time to get on board, to save his soul as his sister had so eloquently put it when she kissed him good bye at the airport.

He turned and faced Uncle Andy. "Professor Cunningham does have a lot of analogies, some quite descriptive."

"Yes, he does," Uncle Andy said. He rose to his feet and moved beside Jason. Looking out across the water, he spoke in a soothing tone. "I've had the privilege of traveling all over the world. Early in my career, I always went to the location at least a day ahead of starting rehearsals to absorb the culture, the energy of the people, so that at the time of the performance I would have a feel for the community around me. I found that very helpful, especially if it was the first time I was in a new venue." A period of silence passed. "When's the last time you did anything spontaneous?" the conductor asked.

Jason let out a huff of air.

"Answers that question, doesn't it?" Uncle Andy said. He paused again. "Today's Thursday. I want you to take the next four days totally off from the piano. I want you to use that time to enjoy this beautiful town, its people, and the sights around it. We'll meet again on Monday, same time, same place."

Don't practice, Jason thought. That wasn't the solution he was figuring on. All his life, the need to practice hard and long had been drilled into him by his instructors. Never had anyone told him to take time off.

Uncle Andy continued. "As I said the first day we met, Jason, I'm a consultant. I evaluate, gather data, and then render an opinion and or suggestions. My opinion, you see things in a singular perspective, and it shows in your play. Let's see if this time off helps."

Jason took a deep breath as he turned and started to pull out his wallet. Uncle Andy laid his hand on his arm. "I got today. You get Monday."

Jason nodded as he put his wallet away. As he did, he couldn't help but stare at the man standing beside him. Jason never imagined when Dr. Cunningham told him he needed to get away that he would end up in such a surreal place, having a conversation with such an esteemed musician as Andrew Summers. The recommendation to take time off certainly wasn't what he expected from the famous conductor. Regardless, Jason had to assume it was good advice, advice from the man with two curio cabinets full of awards.

Saving my soul, Jason thought.

After paying the bill, Uncle Andy turned and faced the lake. "You know Jason, you will enjoy the end result a lot more if you enjoy the journey along the way."

CHAPTER 12

Jason bid Uncle Andy goodbye as the maestro said he was going to the bar to chat with a couple old friends. Jason decided his first order of business was to take a walk along the waterfront. Although still cool, it was a beautiful sunny afternoon. As he kept a fast pace, it wasn't long before he felt his heart rate start to increase. "Much better than a treadmill," he muttered. He went about a mile to where the buildings stopped and the town ended. He then retraced his steps back to the Box On The Dock.

He was about to cross the street when he heard someone call his name. He turned to see Noel opening the side door of the cottage's van. Bear and Louie came bounding out, the big dog almost squashing the little guy in the process. Bear saw Jason and ran toward him. A moment later, Louie was on his heels. Knowing that if he didn't prepare himself there was a chance he'd get knocked over, Jason knelt down and held out his arms. The dogs slowed their pace right before they reached him. However, they didn't slow their eagerness. Back rubs and pets from Jason with licks from the dogs were exchanged.

Noel walked up to them, telling the dogs to behave, which they ignored. Reaching down to give them a couple pets of her own, she said, "They have certainly taken a liking to you."

"I guess that's a good thing," Jason said. Standing up, he gave Noel a gentle hug.

Pulling away, she said, "Anyway, what brings you down here this time of day?"

"I had lunch with Uncle Andy after my session this morning. Then I went for a walk," Jason explained.

"How was lunch?"

"The meatloaf was excellent."

"That's one of my favorites," Noel said.

"What are you doing down here?" Jason asked.

"Uncle Henry called this morning. *My First Lady III* is ready. He winters her at a shipyard up north. Spring has been mild, so the yard was able to get her ready early. Uncle Henry wanted to know if I could go with him to bring her down. His first mate is still in school. I've helped him in the past."

Jason looked toward the water. "Looks like a nice day for a boat ride," he said.

Noel followed his gaze. "Forecast calls for it to get socked in here the next several days. That's one reason why Uncle Henry wants to go today if possible." She paused. "What are your plans the rest of the day?"

"Nothing, actually," Jason said "Uncle Andy wants me to take a couple days off. Sounds strange to me, but I'll give it a try. He thinks I'm too focused on my music."

"You want to come with us?"

"You mean on the boat?"

"We'll go up in the motor skiff and then tow the skiff back," Noel explained.

"Will Uncle Henry mind?" Jason asked. He didn't add

that his boating experience was limited to riding the ferry from Manhattan to Hoboken, New Jersey to eat at one of the several restaurants his family frequented.

"No, he won't mind. The more the merrier," Noel said. "You'll like him, he's a hoot. When he's touring, he's all over the boat, joking with the passengers, making sure everyone has a good time."

"If he won't mind, sounds like fun," Jason said.

The skiff was a 28-foot vintage, refurbished workboat that had been cleaned up and polished for use as a pleasure craft. Uncle Henry was putting some gear on board when they arrived. He looked like a waterman with a tan, weathered face. His hat had the tour boat's name. He wore an old but clean tee shirt and beige coveralls. His footwear consisted of well-broken in boating shoes.

Noel introduced Jason and asked whether he could come along. Uncle Henry welcomed Jason with a firm handshake. Thankfully, he didn't ask any questions about Jason's boating experience. He rubbed the dogs' heads and told them to get their butts on board or he was going to leave them stranded on the pier. Bear jumped onto the skiff without difficulty. Louie yipped until Noel picked him up and carried him aboard. She put him in a doggie life vest, explaining to Jason that he didn't swim very well. Bear, on the other hand, loved the water.

A couple minutes later the engine started, and Noel gave a push off from the pier after untying the lines. Jason and Noel sat on the side seats across from one another. The dogs propped themselves on the back seat and stared off the stern.

They headed diagonally across the lake. After riding for

a few minutes, Uncle Henry pulled back on the throttle. He turned and pointed toward the shore.

"That's Alexander Graham Bell's estate up there on the hill. There are a few other houses as well on the property. If you haven't yet, you really should go see the museum. Bell was involved in a lot more than inventing the telephone."

"I have that on my list of things to do," Jason said, mentally putting it on the list.

They puttered along the shoreline for a few minutes before heading back toward the middle of the lake. A few minutes later, Uncle Henry again slowed the boat.

Pointing toward another area on the shoreline, he said, "I don't think they're here yet but during the summer months, a pair of bald eagles nest there. We bring fish with us when we're on a tour and sometimes they will fly right up to the boat. Makes for a great photograph."

They continued on a northerly route up the lake. Jason continued to look around, mesmerized by the scenery. There were mountains on both shorelines with trees beginning to show signs of summer foliage. There were occasional houses, but mostly the land was untouched. On the starboard, or right side, you could see an occasional vehicle pass along the road that weaved its way beside the lake. The purring of the boat's engine was the only thing that disrupted the tranquility of the area.

Except for pointing out an occasional area of interest, Uncle Henry remained focused ahead. Noel stayed across from Jason, looking around as well. She said little except to also point out an occasional landmark. They continued for an hour or so and then started heading toward the eastern shore. Jason could see a more developed region up ahead. Uncle Henry slowed the boat as they approached a marina with multiple boats docked at a floating pier. There was also a large anchorage area where sailboats of many sizes were moored.

. . . . .

M*y First Lady III* was moored at the end of the pier. She was freshly painted, her name in bold letters across the stern. They pulled up close and moved slowly along her side. "She's looking good," Uncle Henry said as they reached the bow of the double-decker cruiser.

"It's a lot bigger than I expected," Jason said.

"She is that," the boat captain conceded. "She's forty meters...about a hundred and thirty feet. She also looks much larger because we're in a small boat. Put her alongside a ship, then she's not so big."

They pulled into an empty slip, tied up and Uncle Henry cut the engine. "Let me go settle up. You two walk the dogs and get them on board. Noel, check to make sure the batteries are charged, and we have fuel."

"I'll check all the fluid levels, too," Noel said.

"Good. That'll save time."

Uncle Henry went up the pier to find the marina owner. Noel and Jason followed with the dogs taking the lead. A few minutes later, Noel and Jason were back at the boat.

Noel picked up Bear and hugged him with one hand. She explained there was a gangplank used for tours, otherwise...

She pointed to the ladder that ran up the side. She made it up to the first deck slowly, but carefully. She looked down for Louie and saw that Jason had him in a similar hold. She watched Jason closely to make sure he got up okay, which he did after being instructed to take one rung at a time. When they safely on the deck level, Jason sat Louie down.

She gave him a quick tour. The boat was basically two decks. The bottom deck was open on three sides for viewing. Clear, heavy plastic foul-weather curtains could be dropped if needed. The bar and restrooms were along the port side. The deck was open-air so there were plenty of tables and chairs spaced about. The upper deck was similar except the forward part was the pilot house. A wide stairwell near the stern connected the two decks. Noel led Jason below to the engine room. He stopped in the hatchway and watched as she went about checking fluids and other aspects of the machinery.

They then went up to the pilot house. A large, polished, old-fashion ship's wheel took up most of the starboard side. Up on the dash area were a series of instruments. There was a marine radio and other devices bolted to the ceiling that hung down for easy access. In the middle area was a large screen. Noel hit a couple buttons, and the screen flashed a green line before settling into a circular fashion. "That's the radar," Noel explained. "That'll need to warm up before we get underway."

She focused her attention on other instruments and turned on the radio.

They heard Captain Henry climbing the ladder. A moment later, he was in the pilot house with them. He had a handful of papers that he folded and set up on the dashboard.

"According to the guys here, everything is done and in tip top shape." He turned and looked towards Noel. "Everything okay from your end?"

"Oil levels are spot on. Fuel tanks are full. Batteries are charged. Radar is warmed up. Bilge is dry."

"Good work," Uncle Henry said. He looked at Jason. "How about from your end?"

The question caught Jason off guard, but he recovered quickly. "Passengers are all taken care of, sir. Beer's cold. Snacks are ready for consumption."

The boat captain laughed. "You're okay in my book, Jason." Focusing back on the instruments, he added, "Let's get these babies started and warmed up. The weather forecast is for it to remain clear, but the guys up in the office said the weather forecast is for clear skies, but fog is possible later."

Both engines started without difficulty. While they warmed up, Uncle Henry and Noel went about unplugging the shore power, the water hose, and several dock lines. When the thermostats on the engines showed they were getting warm, Uncle Henry announced they were ready to get underway. He stepped to the pier side of the pilot house and called down to Noel, who was preparing to untie the final two lines before she climbed aboard.

"You wanna take her home?" he said. "I'll take the skiff. That way we don't have to tow her, and I can get back and make sure everything's ready at the pier."

Noel didn't hesitate as she dropped the still-attached lines on the pier. "Let's switch places, then," she said. As she climbed the ladder and Uncle Henry started down, she added, "I'll pull out and wait for you to get started. You can give me a radio check before we get underway."

Jason asked if there was anything he could do. Noel said his job was to sit back and enjoy the ride.

After the radio check, Uncle Henry pulled in front of them in the skiff. The boats headed toward home. During this time, Jason remained next to Noel who stood with one hand on the wheel in a relaxed fashion. The dogs plopped down beneath the helm seat for a nap.

"They always take a nap when they first come aboard," Noel said. "I think the vibration from the engines relaxes them."

"I can understand that," Jason said.

Noel laughed. "No napping for the crew."

"Aye, aye, Captain." The remark earned him a poke in the ribs.

Noel spent her time looking in all directions to make sure they didn't have any other boat activity around the marina. She also surveyed the instrument panel regularly, pointing out the skiff on radar.

Jason pointed to a smaller monitor next to the radar which he recognized as a GPS screen. Only instead of landmarks, there were navigational symbols.

"We could almost go home with our eyes closed," he said.

"In theory, that's correct," Noel said. "But that assumes perfect conditions. One of the things you learn out here is that there are no perfect conditions. Things can change quickly and often do. That's why they're called *aids* to navigation."

"So you're a licensed captain, huh?" Jason said.

"I've had my captain's license for three years," Noel

answered. "I go out with Uncle Henry whenever I can, although that's not going to be as much this summer since I'm working more at the cottage."

"I'm impressed," Jason said with sincerity.

Further conversation was interrupted as Captain Henry checked in with them over the radio. "You guys are looking good. Everything okay?"

"Everything's fine," Noel returned.

"Have a safe trip."

"We'll see you at home."

The green dot on the radar slowly moved away.

Noel slid behind Jason and pushed him toward the wheel. "Go ahead and take the helm. There's no significant wind at the moment, so you shouldn't have any difficulty steering. Just hold the wheel loosely." She pointed at the compass. "Try and keep the white line on that course. Then pick a point out ahead and steer toward it. You don't need to be perfect but do the best you can. If you get tired, we'll turn on the autopilot."

Jason hesitated and then put one hand on each of the top two spokes. Noel continued her instructions. "Don't worry about the radar, I'll keep an eye on that for you. Same with the instruments. Focus on steering the boat." She reached over and pushed the throttles forward. "We're past the speed zone around the marina. It'll actually make it easier to steer."

The engines responded immediately, and the boat slowly picked up speed.

Jason said nothing as he focused on the task given him.

CHAPTER 13

Jason quickly got the hang of steering the boat, although it did require him to stay focused on the compass and what was ahead. Noel reminded him to also keep a lookout in all directions to make sure there wasn't anything small the radar wasn't picking up. As Jason relaxed, he was able to take quick glances at the scenery. The area was beautiful in every direction.

Noel initially stood by Jason's side keeping a close eye on the instruments and the water around them. Satisfied he was doing okay, she slid up onto the helm seat behind him. She commented that she never tired of the view, adding, "No matter how many times we go up and down the lake, there is always something different to see."

"Nature's always changing," Jason said. "That's true here in the country as well as in the city."

"I can understand that," Noel said. "Although, it can get a little mundane around here at times, especially in the winter."

"I guess you have to stay spontaneous," Jason said, thinking of his earlier conversation with Uncle Andy.

Noel tipped her head to the side. "That's a good way to put it."

Jason continued to be amazed that they were alone in a large lake in the middle of a large forest nestled in between large mountains. Tranquil. Isolated. Hypnotic. The only sounds were those of the engines, the boat moving effortlessly through the water and the occasional screech of a bird that flew overhead. *What a transformative experience!* Jason thought.

He glanced toward Noel. "Yes, it has been," he almost said aloud.

Noel slid off of her seat. "I'm going to check what surprise package the marina gang left behind the bar. Want anything?"

"You're leaving me?" Jason said nervously, the tranquility quickly dissipating.

"I'm only going to be gone a minute. You'll be fine."

Before Jason could object, she headed toward the steps leading to the lower deck. She returned with a couple bottles of water and packages of cheese and crackers. Opening the waters, she handed one to Jason and took a long swallow from the other. "Want me to take over so you can drink and eat something?"

Jason pointed to the crackers. "That's the surprise package?"

Noel laughed. "There's a bottle of champagne on ice for when we get back."

"I thought that was when a boat was first launched."

"It's a tradition the owner of the marina started years ago. Every time they put a boat in the water, old or new, they leave a bottle of champagne on board. He calls it good luck for a good season."

Noel took another swallow of water as she took a 360-degree visual survey, checked the instruments, and flipped a couple switches halfway down to the floor on the right. Then she again scooted up onto the helm seat Jason had vacated. "We'll let the auto pilot steer for a while." She propped her feet up on the dash. After a drink of water, she said, "You said your father specializes in overseas stocks. What does that mean exactly?"

"Using historical data and current events, he predicts what the various markets are going to do – go up, down, or remain the same. While he does look at individual stocks, he tends to look at the markets as a whole."

"Sounds interesting," Noel said, taking another swallow of water. "Your mother's a fashion designer?"

Jason nodded. "She's been very successful. Her first big break was at a show in New York when one of her gowns received rave reviews. Her second break, the same gown was showcased on the cover of one of the fashion magazines. One thing that has also helped, my sister has developed a name for herself. She targets a younger population and has branched out into business attire as well as formal wear."

Noel paused. "It seems both your parents…and your sister…work in an intense and risky business."

"Your point?" Jason said cautiously.

"Maybe you're following the same pathway with your music."

Failing to hide the defensiveness in his voice, Jason said, "Is that so bad?"

Sensing this, Noel was quick to respond. "Just an observation, Jason. Just an observation."

Jason turned and looked out the side window. He was oblivious to everything around him as he thought about Noel's words. Was he so focused on his music because of his home environment? Or were there other factors involved? He quickly decided it didn't matter. He was who he was. But he could change the path he was on. And that's why he was here in Baddeck.

As he was about to say something to this effect, a strong gust of wind blew through the open windows. Noel looked at him with a smile. "You awoke the wind gods with your thoughts."

"The wind gods?"

"Yes," Noel continued. She pointed toward their right. "Folklore says that the winds begin at a faraway valley and flow over the mountains. They come down across the lake onto the opposite shore. We call them the Winds of Baddeck. They come and go regardless of the weather. No one knows what triggers them, but legend says someone's intense thoughts can bring them on." She tipped her head slightly. "What were you thinking just then?"

"I was thinking about what you said, wondering why I'm the way I am," Jason answered, staring out the window.

"And?"

"That I am a product of my environment."

"That's not a bad thing as long as you understand it," Noel suggested.

Jason turned and looked at Noel. "Kind of what I was thinking as well." He took a drink of his water. "Like I told you, Uncle Andy wants me to take a break from the piano. He wants me to see and enjoy the area. I'm not sure how *not* practicing is going to help," Jason said.

"If you hadn't taken the time off, you wouldn't be here now." Noel said.

After a short pause, Jason said, "Uncle Andy thinks I lack

spontaneity and passion in my life, and that shows in my playing. Technically, he has no issues. Artistically, however…" Jason paused again. "He asked when the last time I did anything spontaneous."

"What was your answer?" Noel queried.

Jason shrugged. "I had none."

Then he smiled and leaned into her. There was a brief hesitation before their lips met. His eyes closed. When their lips parted, his eyes remained closed, taking in her wonderful scent. He was about to pull away when her hand went behind his neck and pulled him to her again. This time their mouths opened. Their tongues met. She pulled him in tighter. Putting his hand behind her neck, he responded in kind. Time stood still, that is until both felt another gust of wind, this one much stronger than previous.

As she gently pushed away, Noel said, "That was certainly spontaneous."

Jason smiled. "It was, wasn't it?"

"It was nice."

"Better than nice," Jason said. Another gust of wind came through the boat. "Does that mean the wind gods approve?"

Noel laughed. She leaned forward and gave him another quick kiss on the lips. As she turned her attention back to the boat, she said, "I'd say they do."

. . . . .

Jason stood next to Noel, close but not touching, except when the boat rocked. Then he would bump into her gently, which she didn't seem to mind. Otherwise, Jason left her alone as he had his own thoughts. The heat sensation that flowed through his body during the kiss remained. It was a pleasant warmth, one he didn't want to escape. He had had an occasional relationship throughout his life, even a couple that lasted several months. Beyond that, he had been free from those burdens. He'd always told himself he didn't have time as he needed to stay focused on his music.

He looked at Noel as he tried to figure out why she was having such an impact on him, stirring up emotions he had never before experienced. He certainly liked her a lot. The question, was there more to it than that? Was he ready for more? After all, he did have a recital to prepare for. Yet....

"What are you in such deep thought about?" Noel asked, breaking his train of thought.

Jason hesitated. "Actually, I was thinking about you; about how nice the kiss was, and how great it is being out on the water with you."

Noel gave him a gentle hip nudge and a smile. "Me, too." The smile faded. A serious expression crossed her face. "You're a wonderful guy, Jason. I like you; I like you a lot. But you're here for a short period of time, then you go back to New York."

"Maybe..." Jason started but stopped when Noel suddenly slid off the helm seat. She leaned forward and stared over the ship's wheel. Her expression changed to one of concern. "Damn."

Before Jason could ask for an explanation, Noel pointed toward a cabinet near the floor. "Grab the binoculars out of there, please."

Jason did as asked.

Pressing the eyepieces to her face, Noel slowly scanned the area forward. "That must be the fog the guys at the marina warned us about," she said. "It looks well delineated and is about a mile ahead."

"What do we do?" Jason asked, not sure whether he should be concerned.

Picking up on his anxiety, Noel answered. "It's nothing to worry about. We just have to slow down and keep a sharp eye out."

Just then the radio squawked, and Uncle Henry's voice came through the speaker. "Do you guys see the fog?"

"Roger that," Noel said. "We just spotted it."

"It rolled in after I passed the area. I didn't see it till I looked behind me. Want me to come back with you?" Uncle Henry offered.

"No sense in both of us getting tangled up in this mess," Noel said. "I'm pulling the throttles back as we speak. I'll call you if there's a problem."

"Roger that. Keep me posted."

Noel hung the microphone back on the clip attached to the radio. She looked at Jason. "It'll just delay our arrival. Why don't you go down and grab some more water and the rest of the crackers before we get into it."

Jason left and was back up at the helm station in a couple of minutes. He opened a bottle of water and handed it to Noel. It wasn't long before they entered the northern side of the fog bank. One moment they could see clearly, the next they were totally engulfed in the mist. Visibility was barely past the bow of the boat.

"Is this common?" Jason asked.

"The fog yes. The density is a bit unusual," Noel replied.

"What can I do?"

"Stand here and keep a sharp eye out."

Jason took a swallow of water. "The wind gods did this, didn't they?"

"I have no doubt," Noel replied.

In thirty minutes or so, they broke free of the fog bank. One moment, they were fogged in. The next moment, they could see clearly, including their destination up ahead. Noel did a visual inspection in all directions and then pushed the throttles forward. The water remained calm with a slight breeze. The sun had fallen behind the mountains but still gave off plenty of light for good visibility.

Noel grabbed the microphone off the radio to call in to her uncle. Before she could say anything, he spoke. "I have a visual on you, Noel. Good work."

"See you in a few," Noel returned. Stepping away from the helm, she said, "You see the end of the pier out there?"

"Yes," Jason replied cautiously.

"Just steer towards that. We've got plenty of time. I'm going to get some fenders and lines ready."

Jason slid into the space behind the wheel. Noel gave him a kiss on the cheek. There was a moment's hesitation and then she kissed him again, this time on the lips. When their lips parted, she said, "Just don't break my heart, okay?"

"I won't, I promise."

CHAPTER 14

When they got back, Jason went right to his room for a nap. He awoke refreshed a couple hours later, took a shower and went down to the bar to eat. As he scooted closer on the stool, Bobby came up with a glass of water. "Want to try a flight of beer for me? We got some samples from a new brewery up north trying to get their product here in town."

"Sure, and a menu, too, please," Jason said taking a long swallow of water.

A short time later, Jason had tasted all five of the samples Bobby had given him. He wasn't a connoisseur of malt beverages, but he gave his opinion nonetheless. As Bobby set a basket of fish and chips in front of him, Jason pointed to the still-full glasses lined up on the wooden board. "I prefer my fruit in a pie." Each of the samples had a different fruity flavor, none of which appealed to Jason.

Bobby laughed. "With a scoop of ice cream." He pulled a set of silverware from beneath the bar. "The flavoring of alcoholic beverages is the new fad."

While eating fish and chips, Jason recapped the afternoon with Noel aboard *My First Lady III*. "While we get fog in the city, it's usually not that thick," he said.

"We get it around here a lot," Bobby said. "Although, we didn't get anything here this afternoon." He capped off Jason's water. "You guys got in okay, right?" Bobby said.

"Noel handled the fog and the boat like a pro," Jason said.

"She is a pro," Bobby said. "Been driving that boat for years."

Jason made no comment.

Which was wise as he failed to see Noel come up behind him. Her hand on his shoulder startled him. "Didn't I teach you anything today? Eyes out in all directions," she said.

Jason gave Bobby a dirty look. "I thought Bobby had my back."

Noel laughed as she slid onto the stool beside him.

"Want anything?" Bobby offered.

She pointed to the small glasses lined up in front of Jason. "Gabbey gave me the night off. She did want me to try the new beers we got in."

A minute later, Bobby slid five sample glasses on a wooden board toward her. Noel raised one of the glasses towards Jason.

"Here's to the newest team member of the Baddeck Boat Delivery Service." She took a sip and instantaneously made an awful face. Sitting the glass down, she tried the next sample with the same result. "These taste like they have fruit in them?"

"Each one's a different flavor," Bobby explained.

She pushed the board away and reached for the water Bobby had also served her. "Not for me," she said. "I prefer my fruit in a pie."

Bobby and Jason looked at one another and broke into a laugh. "With a scoop of ice cream," both spouted simultaneously.

Noel tipped her head to the side. "What's so funny?"

Bobby collected both flight boards, sliding them beneath the bar. "Jason and I said the same," he said.

Noel smiled. “I’ll let Gabbey know.”

Bobby stepped away to greet a new customer at the other end of the bar.

Jason raised his water in a toast. As the glasses touched, he said, “Thanks for inviting me today, and thanks for....” He hesitated.

Noel spoke softly. “Just remember what I said.”

Jason nodded. “I know, no broken hearts.” He didn’t add it could go both ways.

Bobby returned a few moments later, and Jason continued his story. “When we got back, we had champagne to toast our arrival. The shipyard gave us a bottle and guys from The Box On The Dock sent over a couple bottles as well. Everyone that was around – tourists and locals – got a taste. It was really cool.”

“If you stay around here long enough, you’ll find a lot of interesting things,” Bobby said. He looked at Noel who was giving him a stern look. He gave her a wink before moving away.

Noel turned her attention to Jason. “What will you do with the rest of your days off?”

Jason took a long swallow of his water. “I don’t know.” As an afterthought he added. “Maybe I’ll go hang out at the dock and see if I can get another boat ride.”

“You liked that, eh?”

Jason leaned so their shoulders touched. “Yes, I did...eh. I especially liked being with you.”

Noel smiled. “I liked that, too, but ...”

Jason held up his hand. “Let’s not ruin that by worrying about the future.”

Noel's smile widened. "Fair enough." She leaned over and kissed him on the cheek.

As they each sat up straight, they heard Gabbey's voice behind them. "There you are, Jason. I was looking for you. Uncle Andy just called. He has to go to Quebec to fill in for someone who's taken ill. He won't be back by Monday. He said for you to continue with your days off and have some fun."

Jason felt a wave of anxiety. He only had a few months left to prepare for his recital. Didn't Uncle Andy understand that? He swallowed hard. The anxiety subsided as he told himself Uncle Andy probably understood better than anyone. If he felt Jason needed the time off, then who was he to argue?

"You okay?" Noel said, laying her arm on Jason's shoulder.

Jason emptied his water glass and wiped his mouth. "I was just thinking about having more time away from practicing."

"I'm sure Uncle Andy wouldn't have said it if he didn't think it was the right thing to do," Noel said.

"My suggestion," Gabbey said, "is to take advantage of the time, enjoy yourself, and see the sights in the area."

"How?" Jason asked sincerely.

Gabbey pondered the question. "Noel's going to be busy here, so I've asked Alex to take over the local tours. You can tag along with him if you want."

"Okay, just put the cost of the tours on my account."

Gabbey pointed to the piano. "A couple more evenings at the piano and we'll call it even."

Jason smiled. "I think I'm getting the better end of that

deal since I have to practice anyway...once Uncle Andy returns."

"Just have fun and relax," Gabbey directed.

Jason raised his glass. "Thank you."

"Thank you," Gabbey said. "You've added a specialness we haven't seen around the cottage before."

"In that case, since I can't play tonight and can't practice tomorrow..." Jason turned toward Bobby, who was heading in their direction. "Let's get a bottle of champagne and celebrate."

After pulling a bottle out of the cooler and uncorking it in front of the trio, Bobby said, "What's the occasion?"

Holding up his glass in a toast, Jason said, "To the second spontaneous thing I've done today."

CHAPTER 15

Although he didn't drink that much champagne, he awoke the next morning with a slight headache. He took a couple aspirins and drank two glasses of water before taking a shower. He put aside his morning exercise routine as he had to be downstairs by 8:00 o'clock. Alex was taking a family on the Cabot Trail, which would take most of the day.

There were coffee, pastries, orange juice, and a fruit bowl waiting for him and other members of the tour. He took a coffee, a couple of apples, and headed outside to the van. Alex was already there waiting and told him to sit up front with him. Jason got in the van, put on his seat belt and sat back to enjoy his breakfast. A short time later, two families of three joined them. Alex welcomed everyone and gave a brief summary of the day's trip. When everyone was settled, they headed out.

Jason was in awe of the beauty and scenery of the Cabot Trail. Alex was a great tour guide, pointing out various historical areas and facts. There were a couple stops for shopping and bathroom breaks. There were also several pullovers for photographic opportunities and leg stretches. For lunch, Alex suggested Jason wait for their next stop where they were known for their rotisserie chicken. Jason took the advice and was glad he did. They made it back to the cottage in time for dinner. It was then Jason realized he hadn't thought of his music all day.

After saying goodbye to everyone, Jason changed into his workout clothes. He went to the gym figuring he'd get something to eat at the bar later. Adjusting the weights on one of the machines, he said aloud, "Today was a good day...a very good day." He had never heard of the Cabot Trail before coming to Baddeck. Now he felt totally relaxed, something he had not experienced in a long time.

The next day, the destination was Prince Edward Island. Just getting over the bridge onto the island was a sight in itself. The island was famous as the setting for Lucy Montgomery's *Anne of Green Gables,* the story of a little red-headed girl.

Monday's tour was to the Bay of Fundy Park. The area was noted for having the highest tides in the world, up to fifty feet. Alex timed their visit to low tide so they could climb down a set of spiral stairs to walk on the ocean floor.

During the drive back to the cottage, Jason thought about the past three days. He continued to feel relaxed. While he did think about the upcoming recital occasionally, it was no longer foremost on his mind.

CHAPTER 16

The next morning came with clear skies and warm weather. Spring was ebbing into summer with temperatures continuing to rise. Alex and Noel were in the lobby discussing Noel's going to Halifax when Jason passed through on his way to breakfast. He stopped to say hello and Noel asked if he wanted to ride along. As Uncle Andy had yet to return, Jason said yes, he'd like to go. Noel told him to go ahead and eat. She'd get the dogs ready and the shopping lists from everyone. She already had Alex's, which she joked would take up most of the space in the van.

"I'll meet you out back in a few," she said with a soft smile.

Glancing toward the restaurant and seeing a line at the buffet, Jason said, "I'll fix a sandwich and coffee to go. You want something?"

"I'm not hungry, but I will take a coffee," she said. "Just a little cream please."

"A little cream it'll be," Jason said.

Ten minutes later, with Noel at the wheel, the dogs in the back, and Jason riding shotgun, they took off. As they got out on the main road, Noel asked Jason how he was doing not practicing. He commented that he could not remember being so relaxed, adding that the beauty of the area was tranquil and exhilarating.

"How have you been?" he asked. He hadn't seen her much in the past three days.

"Busy," Noel said. "It seems like every time I turn around there's some problem to fix. It's amazing how many different things there are to do in order to run a hotel efficiently and keep the customers happy."

"Isn't that what you're supposed to be learning?" Jason asked.

"Yes, but none of the textbooks teach us about all the little things" Noel said. She took a sip of coffee. "You're a customer, what do you think so far?"

"Everything and everyone have been wonderful," Jason said. He led out a soft chuckle. "If I had any criticism, it's that Louie and Bear are a little sloppy with their tongues."

Hearing their names, both dogs woke up and stuck their heads on the middle armrest. Jason laid his hand atop Bear's head. Bear immediately started licking his wrist. Louie nudged his way into the act as well. Rubbing them both firmly, Jason said, "I was only kidding guys. I was only kidding."

As the highway increased in elevation, Noel said, "There's a good place to pull over up ahead and let the dogs out. There's a small gift shop that has all kinds of quirky things. It's also a beautiful view, if you want to take some photos."

Jason had never been much of a picture-taker, but since arriving in Canada he'd certainly taken advantage of his cell phone's camera, including taking several selfies with Noel. He'd sent some pictures to his parents and sister, who all told him they were pleased he was exploring the area. No one asked who the beautiful girl with him was, though.

As promised, the view from the rest stop was spectacular, and the dogs especially liked the treats the owner of the store had ready for them."

Inside the store, Jason bought several gifts to take to his family, including a small hand-painted, ceramic moose. Tucked away in one corner sat an elderly woman working on a hook rug. Numerous examples of her work were displayed on the walls behind her. Noel told Jason that rug-making was one of many art forms fading out with the older generation.

Back in the van, Jason set his feet up on the dash. Bear's head lay on the center armrest and Louie was in Jason's lap. Noel looked over, shook her head to the side, and said, "Now if that isn't a sight to see."

Jason handed her his cellphone, and she took several pictures of the trio. The photos turned out quite well and would later be some of Jason's favorites from the summer.

They made it to the Halifax Walmart without difficulty. Gabbey had taken the lists from Noel before they left and faxed in the order. There was a palette with supplies sitting on one of the docks with the cottage's name on it.

"They certainly make it easy," Jason said. "Just like the time I was here with Alex."

"It's all about customer service, eh," Noel said.

Noel backed the van up to the loading dock. As they opened the rear doors, a couple of young boys came out and helped them load the supplies. Bear and Louis stayed in the van supervising, making sure everything was in its place and that there was room left for them. It was a tight fit, but they did get everything loaded and secured.

From there, Noel drove down to the waterfront and parked in an open-air public lot.

"We have some time. I thought you might like to see the Halifax Boardwalk," she said. "The boardwalk runs along the waterfront. It's dog-friendly, and there are plenty of places to choose for lunch."

They started at the north end and took a leisurely stroll south. Jason took in the sights, taking pictures of the harbor as they went. As Alex had mentioned during Jason's first visit to Halifax, the boardwalk was a combination of store fronts, restaurants, and food stands. Several hotels were mixed in as well.

"What's a lobster roll?" Jason asked after they passed several places advertising the same.

"You've never had a lobster roll?" Noel said somewhat surprised.

"Can't say that I have."

"Well, we'll fix that."

They ate at one of Noel's favorite restaurants on the outside deck that overlooked the harbor. Bear and Louie sat under the table and watched the people as they passed by. An occasional dog came by to say hello as well. The lobster roll was delicious. Jason would later describe it as a lobster salad sub. Noel smiled as she watched Jason take the last bite. "Have you ever had lobster before?" she asked.

"Lobster plenty of times, but never like this," he admitted. "It's one of the most delicious new foods I've had here – right up there with fish stew and meatloaf."

Noel laughed. "I'm glad you like it."

Jason scanned the scenery, his eyes stopping on Noel. "It's beautiful here, especially with you being in the picture." He took his cellphone and took several shots of Noel with the harbor in the background. They finished their meal in silence.

As they settled the dogs in the van, Noel said, "We have time for one more stop."

A few blocks later, she made a right turn into what took Jason a moment to realize was a cemetery. Noel pulled into an empty spot in the visitor's parking lot. She exited the van and let the dogs out. They took off to do their business.

"I can't show you the exhibits in the museum they have in town; it's not dog friendly," Noel said. "But we can walk around here a bit. It's where many of the *Titanic* victims are buried."

"I know about the *Titanic*," Jason said. "I didn't realize Halifax was so historically attached to the tragedy."

"Halifax citizens were some of the first to respond," Noel explained.

There was a map of the cemetery and a bronze plaque listing those buried. They walked forward, slowly and quietly. Jason noticed the sudden change in atmosphere. The hustle-bustle of the city had suddenly become quiet. They entered the area where the victims of the *Titanic* were buried. Some had names and dates. Other markers simply had the sex of the person. There were even children's graves, again some with names, some without.

Noel spoke as they walked hand in hand. "I always considered the *Titanic* tragedy symbolic of mankind's rush to get ahead. As part of our First Nation education, we're taught that one should keep a gentle pace with life, listen to nature and live in synchronicity with the environment."

Stopping before one of the markers, Jason said, "The *Titanic's* captain should have listened to the ice gods."

"You're right, one should listen to what nature is saying," she said softly, as she leaned into him.

A short time later, they turned and went back to the van. Bear and Louie were there waiting. When everyone was again loaded, Noel headed out of the cemetery in the direction of the bridge that would take them over the harbor toward home.

CHAPTER 17

Back at Baddeck Cottage, the staff helped unload the van. When everything was properly stored, Jason thanked Noel for inviting him to go with her. Anytime spent with her was a gift. Noel had similar thoughts.

Jason decided to have dinner at the bar and ordered a burger that proved to be excellent. Bobby suggested a pairing with a wine from one of the local vineyards. That too was excellent.

As Bobby cleared the dishes and refilled Jason's wine glass, the bartender nodded toward a group of people at the far end of the bar. "They heard we had a pianist and asked what time he was going to play."

"I'm still on my sabbatical," Jason said.

Wiping down the bar, Bobby said, "I guess that's good for you, bad for them."

"Sorry," Jason said.

Before Jason could say anything else, he felt a hand on his shoulder. He turned to see Noel standing behind him. Hellos were exchanged as she slid up onto the stool next to him.

"The group down there asked if there was going to be music tonight?" Jason said.

"Is there?"

"Not my choice," Jason said.

"It is your choice," Noel corrected. "You're *choosing* to follow Uncle Andy's advice."

"I'm certainly enjoying my time off. Like I've said, I feel more relaxed than I've been in years. I just hope it improves my performance."

Noel gave him a gentle shoulder rub. "Let's hope for the best."

Gabbey's arrival interrupted any further conversation. Her expression told Noel this was not a *sit and chat time.* "What's up?" Noel said.

Gabbey leaned up against the bar. "Margaret Williams called out. Evidently her sister had a stroke. Margaret's on her way to Halifax Hospital. She asked if someone could check on her dogs tomorrow. She gave them plenty of food and water before she left so they should be okay until then. I told her not to worry and go see to her sister."

Noel looked at Jason. "Margaret works in housekeeping. She's been with the Baddeck Cottage for years. She's a hard worker, and everyone loves her." Turning to Gabbey, Noel continued, "I'll run up to her cabin tomorrow afternoon. Her dogs aren't always the friendliest, but I know them, and they know me. They also get along well with Bear and Louie."

"Want some company?" Jason asked without hesitation.

Looking at Jason, Gabbey said, "Margaret Williams lives in a log cabin almost at the top of the mountain behind us. It's rugged, even by our standards."

"Another adventure, eh?" Jason said with a shrug.

"The company 'll be nice," Noel said. "Plus, you can see how rugged Canadians live."

Gabbey gave them each a pat on the back before heading back to the lobby.

Finishing his wine, Jason said, "What do I need to bring?"

"Do you have hiking boots?" Noel inquired.

"No."

"There's an outdoor store in town. We'll go after breakfast in the morning and get you everything you might need." She paused. "I'd pack an overnight bag as well. You never know up there."

"How rustic is it?" Jason said, failing to hide his sudden apprehension.

"The cabin is wonderful. She got electric hooked up a couple years ago and running water via a well pump system. The issue is getting there. The road up the mountain stops two miles from her place. From there, it's all a dirt road, which isn't always in the best condition."

"Margaret works every day?" Jason asked.

"Seldom calls out. If the snow's too bad, she comes to work on a snow mobile."

"Wow!"

"When you live up here, you learn to adapt," Noel said.

. . . . .

Noel planned to leave for the cabin by mid-afternoon. It was a thirty-minute ride, assuming the roads were okay, giving them plenty of time to check on the animals and get back down the mountain road before it was too dark. After breakfast, Noel and Jason drove to the outdoor store in town where he bought a pair of hiking boots along with a couple pairs of shirts and hiking shorts. When he was finished, he modeled his new clothes for Noel. She laughed, telling him he looked good, but still looked like a tourist.

"You're boots are new so you'll have to look out for blisters, but hopefully we won't be doing all that much walking," Noel said.

When they were heading back to the cottage, she told Jason she spent a lot of time hiking. "Whenever there's a tour group that wants to go hiking, Gabbey sends me," she said. "She trusts me the most not to get lost."

Jason started to laugh but cut the gesture short. "What kind of wildlife are we likely to encounter?"

"Deer...rabbits...moose...bears."

"Bears?"

"Don't worry, they're harmless...usually," Noel said.

"Usually?"

She stopped walking and turned toward him. "Jason, we're in the mountains. What do you expect?"

"Quite frankly, I don't know what to expect."

"Hopefully we won't have too many surprises," Noel said. "We will spray ourselves good with insect repellent to help with the flying kind of wild animals."

"Whatever," Jason said.

The trip to Margaret William's cabin was uneventful with no wildlife encounters. The ride up the dirt road was rough, but Noel's Jeep Wrangler took the terrain in stride. Jason held on with one hand, the other wrapped around Louis who was in his lap. Bear found a spot among the gear in the back. Both animals slept most of the way, only becoming alert as they approached the cabin. Noel stopped the Jeep and stepped out so Bear could get out. Louie was right on his heels. Noel got back in quickly and closed the door.

Just as quickly, she explained. "I always let Bear and Louis out first to go find Margaret's dogs so they can recognize one another. Makes them less aggressive. Once they get to know you, they're very friendly, and very protective."

"I guess that's good for this type of environment," Jason commented.

"Margaret has them well trained."

"They know you, but they don't know me," Jason said cautiously.

"You stay here a minute," Noel directed. After a couple more minutes, she exited the Jeep where she moved to and sat on the porch steps. Within moments, four dogs came tearing around the side of the cabin, tails wagging as they did zoomies around one another. Margaret's dogs were mixed breeds, having been rescued from one of the animal shelters in the area. The larger one, the male, was named Walter. The female was Suzy. They saw Noel on the porch at about the same time. Their happiness was set aside as they stood with tails up, teeth partially exposed. Each emitted a soft growl. Noel sat still, letting the dogs get her scent. When recognition was established, their demeanor changed, and they were all over her, happy to see an old friend. A moment later, Bear and Louie joined in the fray.

After a few pats, hugs and licks, Noel grabbed a hold of Bear and pointed toward the Jeep. "Go introduce your friends to Jason," she commanded.

Bear understood, barked his acknowledgment and took off toward the vehicle. The other three followed. A short time later, four dogs and two humans were playing on the porch. Eventually, the dogs gave off a few barks, and the pack took off around the back of the cabin.

The cabin was a well-maintained one-story log dwelling, much larger than Jason had expected. There were flower beds on each side of the porch, which ran the full front of the house. Wooden chairs and tables were set about. An old-fashion swing hung from chains on one side. Inside, the cabin had a very rustic feel.

"The place is very nice," Jason said, setting a couple bags on the kitchen counter. "A lot more modern than I would have thought. Although, I imagine living here in the winter can be tough."

"In can be if you're not used to the winter weather. Otherwise, per Margaret, it's just another day in paradise," Noel said.

"You all are a much hardier bunch than me," Jason said with a laugh. He headed out to the Jeep for more bags.

While Noel was checking the cabin and putting the supplies away (they had brought a few extra groceries for Margaret), Jason went out back to feed and water the dogs. He watched the animals devour the food a few moments while taking in the scenery behind the house. The mountain rose above them. While they were near the top, they were not at its peak. Just like everywhere else he'd seen on this trip, the scenery was beautiful.

Once Noel had everything put away, she met Jason on

the front porch where he was entertaining the four dogs. A quick survey of his clothing showed that *entertaining* included rolling around on the ground.

She sat down beside him. Handing him a bottle of water and an apple, she said, "Alex always does a more thorough inspection when he comes up here. He likes to stay ahead of any maintenance problems. I did a quick look around and didn't see any issues."

"It's good that you all keep an eye on this place for Margaret," Jason said.

"We do our best."

Jason took a long swallow of water and a bite of his apple. He wiped his chin with his sleeve.

"You're going to mess up your new cloths, eh," Noel teased.

Jason started to say something, then stopped. Instead, he grabbed and wiped his mouth on Noel's arm.

She laughed as she pulled away, wiping her arm on her shorts. "I don't know who's worse, you or the dogs."

"Let's call it a tie," Jason said. He leaned toward her. Their lips met, parted, and then met again.

Jason was about to put his arm around Noel's neck when her phone buzzed. She pulled her cellphone from her back pocket. Seeing it was Gabbey, she mouthed the name to Jason. "What's up, Auntie?" she asked.

"Take a look down the mountain," Gabbey directed.

Noel stood up and looked past the Jeep. She seldom used profanity. Today was an exception.

"What's the matter?" Jason said, standing up beside her.

Noel pointed toward the road leading up to the cabin.

"What the devil is that?" Jason said.

"Remember when we were out on the boat the other day how the fog came off the mountain and rolled across the water to the opposite shore?" Noell said. "Well, now the winds are pushing it onto the shore, through town and right up toward us." She paused for a moment. "It looks thick and nasty."

Realizing she still had Gabbey on the line, she put the phone back to her ear. "We see it. Don't know if we're going to get through it or not." She paused for a second. "Have you heard anything from Margaret?"

"She called a little while ago from the hospital. Her sister is stable. Margaret's going to stay at least overnight. She'll keep me posted."

"What do you have for me to do tomorrow?" Noel asked.

"A Cabot Trail tour, but I can get Alex to do that," Gabbey replied.

Noel was comfortable with fog on the water. On the side of a mountain, there were too many chances to run off the road and get into trouble. Noel glanced at Jason as she said, "I think we'll stay here tonight." She looked at Jason who nodded his agreement.

"I think that's a good decision," Gabbey said.

. . . . .

Noel made a snack of cheese and crackers while Jason grabbed a couple cans of birch beer soda (another first for him) from the ice chest they had brought. They sat on the porch swing with the dogs off to the side. It wasn't long before the fog surrounded them, absorbing what light was left. Soon they couldn't see anything past the porch. Even the dogs, who had moved to the other side of the porch, looked blurry. All four of them were lying side by side, heads facing forward, sound asleep. The only sounds were from the light wind rustling its way through the trees, and the chains squeaking rhythmically on the swing.

Noel took a sip of her soda and looked at Jason. "So tell me, has your trip here been worth it?"

"Most definitely," Jason said. He leaned into her. Their lips met. The kiss was long and passionate. When they parted, Jason added, "Meeting everyone, especially you, has been wonderful. I can honestly say I feel relaxed. However, I still have to keep in mind why I'm here. I won't know the effect all this will have until I sit back down at the piano."

"Hopefully, it will all be positive," Noel said as she kissed him again.

They sat in silence. When Noel's soda was finished, she said, "Let's go inside and see what we can fix for supper."

CHAPTER 18

Supper, as Noel called it, consisted of homemade vegetable soup and buttermilk biscuits brought from the cottage. There was also a bottle of red wine and cheesecake for dessert. Jason cleaned up the dishes and put out more food and water for the dogs. Margaret's dogs stayed outside in a doghouse/shelter in the back. Bear insisted on going with them, but Noel wanted Louie inside, explaining that if the pack took off into the woods during the night, he might not be able to keep up and could subsequently get lost.

"Why would they go into the woods at night?" Jason queried.

"They're going to chase anything they consider a threat," Noel explained.

"Anything such as?"

Noel laughed at Jason's concerned expression. "There are a few coyotes in the area. There're also bears. Mostly though, it's just moose roaming around."

Jason's mouth opened and then closed.

"Don't worry, the dogs will keep them away."

Jason finished cleaning up without comment, not wanting to further show his naivety or concern. He couldn't remember ever sleeping anywhere where he was in danger of being eaten by a bear.

While Jason finished in the kitchen, Noel took the

sleeping bags into the extra bedroom and started making up the bunk beds. "You want top or bottom?" she shouted out.

"Huh?"

"Top bunk or bottom bunk?"

"Oh…I wouldn't know, I've never slept in bunk beds."

Noel clicked her tongue against her teeth a couple times. "You take the bottom. I wouldn't want you to fall out of bed."

Jason had walked into the bedroom. "Want me to sleep out in the living area or something?"

"No different than if we're outside in a tent. We're adults, aren't we? But if you want, you can sleep in the Jeep."

The image of being attacked by a hungry bear returned. "Bottom bunk is fine."

"I'm going to go take a shower in Margaret's bathroom. You can use the hose outside if you want. Give me ten minutes before you take yours. Water pressure can sometimes be a little fickle, eh."

Jason glanced at his watch and gave her a smirky grin. "Clock's ticking...eh."

She slapped him on the shoulder, grabbed her overnight kit and headed across the cabin.

. . . . .

Jason waited ten minutes before going outside. He found the hose neatly coiled in an old fashioned wash pan. Chuckling, he muttered, "Another first."

Back in the extra bedroom, he dressed in a pair of gym shorts and an old tee shirt. The temperature in the cabin was comfortable, but without air-conditioning, the humidity remained high. He smiled again. "Such sacrifices I'm making."

"How was your shower?"

Noel's voice startled him. He spun to find her standing in the doorway of the bedroom. She was dressed in shorts and an extra-long T shirt. Her hair was wrapped in a towel. Jason could only stare. "The shower was great," he said. "Thanks. How was yours?"

"You waited the ten minutes like I asked."

"Yes, I did."

As Jason stared at Noel, the continual question of why he was so attracted to her rose to the surface. She was beautiful, yes; but again, he had been around beautiful women before. Then again, he never expected to be sitting on a log cabin porch atop a mountain in the wilderness of Canada next to a First Nation girl, a girl he was....

"What are you looking at and thinking about?" Noel said, interrupting his thoughts.

Seconds passed. "You and you," Jason finally said. He braved taking a step toward her. He paused before another step. "I don't know how I've been so lucky to end up here with you. You are just so...so beautiful...inside and out." Taking another step closer, "I know it's only been a short time, but Noel Summers, I'm..." He hesitated. "I'm falling in love with you."

They kissed. They kissed again. When they broke apart after the third time, Jason said softly into her ear, "I have never said that to anyone before."

"I've never had anyone say that to me before either," Noel said just as softly.

. . . . .

Noel's head began to spin. Memories of previous summer romances with a broken heart came into focus. Did she want to risk that happening again? She admitted she had strong feelings for Jason. But was she ready to let him know that? Was she ready to open herself up for a third time? How many times can one's heart be broken?

She took a deep breath. "Jason…."

His finger came across her lips. "I know, summer romances and all that," he said. "But I promise you this, whatever we have will never be just a summer romance."

"Then what will it be?" Noel said, her curiosity stirred. She kissed him gently on the neck.

"I can only tell you what I wish for at this particular moment."

"I'm listening."

Jason's head tilted as he gave her a half-smile. Without taking his eyes off her, he said, "My wish is to wake up beside you tomorrow morning, hugging you, and saying as we kiss, 'That was the best night of my life.'" Pausing, he added, "Do you have a wish?"

More silence followed as Noel's mind continued to churn. Was she ready for this? Too soon? Too fast? Two deep breaths and she spoke softly, "My wish is that you would say something just like that."

. . . . .

They lay in the lower bunk; each having slept soundly once they went to sleep. Jason was on his side, watching as her chest rose and fell with each breath. Her hair was spread out on the pillow with one strand across her face. She seemed to be at peace. He certainly knew he was.

As he reached to push the strand away, her eyes opened. She smiled. Her arms came away from her side and went around his neck. She pulled him to her. Their lips met. "Good morning," she said when they parted. "You sleep okay?"

He kissed her once and then kissed her again. "That was the best night of my life," he said.

Her smile widened. "It was for me, too." Another kiss and she continued. "Want to make it the best morning of our lives as well?"

Jason smiled as he untangled his feet from hers. Pulling her on top of him, he said, "Let's find out."

By mid-morning, the fog had cleared. The sky held only a few lingering clouds. The temperature was warming rapidly, indicating it was going to be a hot, sticky day.

. . . . .

While Jason was outside tending to the dogs, Noel fixed breakfast. While she did, she checked in with Gabbey. Margaret had called Gabbey earlier and said her sister was stable, but she would like to stay another day. Gabbey had already asked Alex to come up. As he had been up to the cabin numerous times in the past, the dogs were familiar with him. Noel said she'd leave Bear behind just to be sure. Louie wouldn't like this, but he'd get over it. Bear, on the other hand, would be happy to spend another day romping around in the woods with his buddies.

The ride down the mountain two hours later was quiet. Noel focused on driving and on avoiding the many potholes. Jason held on with one hand, firmly holding Louie in his lap with the other. The dog was fast asleep, oblivious to the bouncing of the vehicle, exhausted from the past day's activities.

Noel pulled into the back of the cottage where they unloaded their gear. As they parted ways, Noel grabbed Jason's hand. She looked deep into Jason's eyes. "Just remember your promise, okay?"

Jason smiled. "Not just a summer romance." He leaned in and kissed her lightly on the lips. "You remember something, also." Noel gave him an inquisitive look. "Wishes can come true," he said smiling.

CHAPTER 19

The bar area was busy that evening as the tourists who had arrived earlier had finished their dinner and were now continuing to socialize with one another. Bobby moved back and forth like a well-choreographed dancer. While he had little time to talk, he did make sure the beer glass in front of Jason remained filled. As Jason was watching the bartender intently, he failed to notice Noel, who had come up beside him.

"What are you looking at?" she asked, draping an arm across his shoulder.

Jason gave her a kiss on the cheek. "Just watching Bobby work the crowd."

"He has probably doubled the bar tabs of everyone here just with his personality and looks," Noel said. "Especially with the unattached ladies."

Bobby came by, saving Jason from having to respond. "Evening boss. Want something to drink?"

Noel could only laugh. Pointing to Jason's glass, she said, "I'll have whatever he's drinking."

Bobby nodded and moved away.

When her beer arrived, she took a sip. "Is this another new one we're trying?"

"Bobby said it's a local brewer's summer ale," Jason answered.

Noel took another sip. "Not bad." Turning to Jason, she said, "So what's your schedule the next couple of days?"

"As it's been lately, nothing planned," Jason said. He took a long swallow of his beer. Wiping the foam from his mouth, he continued. "My vacation, or whatever you want to call it, with Uncle Andy will be over on Friday; then I get back to work."

"You seem to be doing okay with the time off."

"This has been the longest I've been away from the piano since I started playing. At first, I was concerned and felt like I was abandoning my music. As time goes on, I've enjoyed not having to practice. I never minded practicing, but the pressure to do so was always a weight on my shoulders, even if it was self-imposed." He took another drink of beer. "I do feel more at ease. I'm having more fun. And..." He paused as he continued to stare at her. "I've met a beautiful woman who has turned everything in my life upside down."

Her hair was pulled in a ponytail with a couple strands falling across to her forehead. He reached up and pushed them away. It reminded him of when he awoke that morning.

Kissing him on the cheek, Noel said, "The feeling is mutual." She turned and looked across the room at the crowd. "Anyway," she added, "I was wondering if you wanted to take a ride with me tomorrow?"

"Where are we going?"

Noel smiled. "Just meet me out back tomorrow morning at 9:00 am."

"Okay," Jason said. "Are we hiking somewhere?"

"No. Casual attire is fine."

"9:00 am it is."

. . . . .

Jason was ready and waiting the next morning right on time. Noel came out carrying a large gray storage box. "Need help?" Jason offered.

"There're a couple more boxes right inside the door. Grab one. I'll get the other," Noel said, sliding the box she carried into the back of the cottage's van.

As the boxes were loaded, Louie came dashing around the corner. Jason lifted him up and climbed into the front passenger seat. He was trying to put the dog in the back, but Louie would have none of it. Jason's lap was his preferred seat.

They were underway a minute later. The sky was clear, the temperature in the mid-seventies. There was no breeze, although the winds were forecasted to increase throughout the day as thunderstorms were predicted for later in the afternoon.

They left Baddeck without a problem. Miles passed in silence. Jason continued his survey of the countryside, noticing as he had before that there were sporadic houses along the road, each well maintained. He wondered what it would be like to live in such a far-out location, especially in the winter. Simple logistics of going to the store had to be much more difficult than what he experienced by walking out the door of his building and into a food store a block away.

He glanced over at Noel, wondering what she would think after a visit to the city. She told him she had never been outside of Canada, and that Halifax was the largest city she had ever visited. Her life experiences were so different from his. He'd like to know more about her, but….

The thought stopped, and he chuckled.

Hearing this, Noel said, "What's so funny?"

"I was just thinking."

"About?"

Jason hesitated. "Normally, I'm a cautious person. Lately, however...."

"Are you having regrets?" Noel asked with concern.

Jason looked at her and smiled. "Not at all."

"I'm glad," Noel said. "I would hate to think..."

Jason laid his hand on her thigh and gave it a squeeze.

"Jason, I'm driving here!"

"Yes, you are. And I'm thinking positive thoughts, not negative ones."

She laid her free hand atop his. "Thank you." She squeezed his hand. "It's nice feeling good about being touched."

"Noel," Jason said, "you're touching me in more ways than one."

"The feeling's mutual."

. . . . .

Time passed with conversation remaining light as Jason continued watching the scenery. They did stop once to let Louie out and to stretch their legs. Ahead of them was a sign that read twelve kilometers to Millbrook. "We're almost there," Noel said.

"What's in Millbrook?" Jason asked.

"You'll see," Noel answered solemnly.

A short time later, they pulled into a gravel parking

lot in front of a largish, plain-looking building with a sign reading "Millbrook Cultural & Heritage Centre." The word "Mi'Kmaq" appeared in smaller letters.

Jason's eyes widened. "Is this an Indian reservation?"

"Yes," Noel said.

A thought suddenly crossed Jason's mind. "Are we going to meet your family?"

Noel continued looking straight ahead. "My mother, yes. It's not something I've ever done with anyone before," Noel said softly.

"I'm honored."

Jason said nothing more as he and Louie exited the passenger side. The dog ran around the front of the van to Noel's side where he led them into the visitors' entrance. Jason stood back as Noel greeted and hugged various staff members as they came up to her. She knew everyone. The group parted as an older, gray-haired, short, stout woman stepped forward. She looked completely surprised. She said nothing as she hurried forward and gave Noel a hug,

"You should have called to let me know you were coming," the woman said.

"I wanted it to be a surprise, Mother," Noel said, giving her another hug.

The woman stepped back and gave her daughter a good up-and-down look. Before she could say anything, Noel reached back and grabbed Jason by the arm, pulling him up beside her.

"Mother, I'd like you to meet Jason Kinde. He's a guest at the cottage, and I've been showing him the sites."

Noel's mother did a second visual inspection before she smiled and extended her hand. "It's a pleasure to meet you, Mr. Kinde. I hope you're enjoying your stay at the cottage, and I hope you enjoy your visit to our Heritage Center."

Jason took her hand. "Your daughter has been a great friend and a wonderful guide."

A couple of the young female staff members took it upon themselves to interrupt the conversation before Jason was put on the spot.

One winked at Noel as she said to Jason, "I think we should get going on your tour as we are expecting a couple large tours shortly." She took Jason's arm and headed toward the first exhibit. Looking over her shoulder, she said, "Go ahead and spend time with your mother, Noel. We'll take care of Jason."

Jason did indeed get the VIP tour. It seemed that every young female staff member was part of the entourage. As he looked at the exhibits and listened to what they were saying, he casually asked how they all knew Noel. He had to hold back a laugh as four out of five said they were cousins. The fifth girl was one of Noel's best friends. All were young First Nation women.

Jason was fascinated by the First Nation people and their history as he tried to absorb as much information as possible. It was enlightening to learn about Noel, her upbringing, and her heritage. Bringing him here was showing him her soul.

Noel's mother was waiting for him in the lobby as the tour finished. The tour guides led him to the middle of the floor. Noel's mother told him to stand still and relax.

"Nothing bad is going to happen to you," she reassured him softly.

Jason did as he was told. As the five tour guides formed a circle around him, Noel stood off to the side. Her mother held a small ceramic pot. She took out a few wooden sticks that were smoking. The smoke had a mild incense-like scent. Noel's mother gently waved them up and down and around Jason. Her lips moved in silence. The room became quiet.

The ceremony was short. Noel's mother put the sticks back in the pot and stepped away. She looked at Noel and said something in her native tongue. She then focused on Jason. "The people of the First Nation welcome you, Jason Kinde. We hope you have enjoyed your visit and hope to see you again. May you continue to enjoy your stay at the Baddeck Cottage," she paused, "and continue to enjoy the time spent with my daughter."

. . . . .

Noel and Jason spent a few more minutes with the staff, Noel making sure she spoke to everyone. After she said good-bye and kissed her mother, they all walked outside. Her mother said something to Noel in her native language before walking back inside. As Jason lifted Louie into the van, he noted the boxes in the back had been unloaded.

Jason saw Noel had tears in her eyes. Handing her a couple of the tissues he found in the glovebox, he said, "Happy tears or sad tears?"

Taking the tissues, Noel said, "Visits with my family, especially my mother, are always too short."

"We could have stayed longer if you wanted," Jason said.

"My mother is the manager of the center, and they have a busy day scheduled."

"We'll just have to come again," Jason said matter-of-factly.

Making sure there was no traffic around them, Noel took a quick glance toward him. "You would do that?"

"Noel, introducing me to your mother and your culture was special," Jason said. "You said you've never done that before." After a moment's hesitation, "Did they like me?"

"The girls thought you were a doll," Noel teased. After a breath and with a more serious tone, "My mother said you seemed nice, and she would like to get to know you better. And, Jason, that's a compliment coming from my mother."

"Even more of a reason to go again. And yes, I would do that for you and your mother…and for me," Jason said. He looked out the window as he rubbed Louie's back. "The center is fascinating. You get a condensed history course walking through the displays."

"That you can," Noel agreed.

"Back to your mother," Jason said. "Did she say anything specific about me?"

"She liked that you took a serious interest in the center and what it had to offer. Everyone liked the fact that you participated in the smudging session without a lot of questions beforehand. She did comment that you were not First Nation."

"Is that a problem?" Jason asked. It was the first time he had thought about this.

"Not from my mother. She was more concerned about your family's reaction."

Jason failed to hold back a chuckle as he grabbed her hand. "My family will fall in love with you quicker than I did."

Noel let out a breath and smiled.

"The smudging…its purpose?" Jason asked.

"It's a cleansing ritual," Noel explained. "The smoke attaches to the negativity in your body and takes it away. That my mother performed the ceremony herself is an indication of her high opinion of you."

Jason's eyes widened. "Then I definitely want to go back so I can thank her."

"She would like that."

As they drove through Noel's hometown, Jason asked about Millbrook's population. Noel told him it was a little over two thousand. When asked why she was working at the cottage instead of in Millbrook, Noel said, "I've already worked at the cottage for several summers. Plus, my internship requires experience at a facility larger than anything on the reservation…at least any place here at the present."

Jason picked up on the second part of the comment. "Are there plans for the future?"

"The Council, the group that runs the town, has debated bringing gambling to the reservation. Everyone seems to be against it at the moment, but you never know what the future holds. The town is doing okay financially, but again, tomorrow may be a different story. Reservations that have casinos make a lot of money. They also have a lot of problems, problems we've been able to avoid. I'd like to see the town focus more on being a place where you can bring your whole family and enjoy the activities and the historical aspects of the area."

"How does your mother feel about casinos?" Jason asked.

"She's hardcore against them because of the trouble they bring. She watched..." Noel paused and let out a deep sigh as tears formed. Dabbing her eyes with one hand, Noel continued. "My father went to work at a reservation casino further north for better pay and benefits. Which was fine except he couldn't avoid the opportunity to get into trouble with alcohol. By the time he accepted he had a problem, it was too late. His liver was shot." Noel paused again. "It's a terrible way to die."

"I'm so sorry," Jason said. "How long ago did he die?"

"Almost six years ago."

"Any brothers or sisters?" Jason asked.

"One older brother. He works at the same casino as my father. I think he wants to prove he can handle the temptation of the environment. He took my father's death hard because he watched the man he loved destroy himself, and there was nothing he, or any of us, could do."

"The sense of guilt is hard to overcome," Jason said.

"That it is," Noel agreed. "But my brother's doing okay. While he does have a drink occasionally, it's rare." She paused. "It's hard because he's away so much. We miss him, and I think he misses us."

"Then you're your mother's closest support," Jason commented.

"First Nation people take care of each other. I do what I can. Those around her do the same."

A period of silence followed before Jason said, "I do have a couple questions. Your mother said something to you in your native language. Can you share?"

Noel nodded. "She reminded me that there are two important things in life. First is to understand where you've come from. The second is to understand where you are today. The assumption is that these two will help you make better decisions for the future. The Heritage Center is a reminder of this."

"Do you understand where you are today?" Jason said. "I'm not sure I know the answer to that about myself."

"Isn't that why you came to Baddeck – to find your inner soul?"

"I'm finding a lot more than that," Jason chuckled. After a brief pause. "What about you. Where are you today?"

"Not so long ago, I was struggling with issues, including my father's death. First Nation people are taught to be strong, so I buried those issues as I focused on my work at the cottage and school. Now, those emotions have resurfaced with a whole new set of feelings."

"Because of me?" Jason said.

"I've let you into my life, Jason, in a way never before," Noel replied. "It's new. It's exciting. I just need to be careful." She paused as a truck passed them. "I think we both need to be careful with ourselves, and with each other."

"Then why bring me up here today?" Jason said.

"I wanted you to see where I've come from."

"Were you concerned about my reaction?"

"A girl is always concerned when she takes someone to meet her family the first time, our culture differences aside."

They drove a few miles in silence. "You want to know how I really feel?" Jason said.

Noel nodded her head yes.

"Okay…Find somewhere to pull over," Jason directed with a serious tone.

"What?"

"Just pullover somewhere."

There was a scenic overlook a short distance ahead which Noel pulled into. Fortunately, they had the spot to themselves. It was quite a picturesque view over a series of farms. Jason got out of the van and let Louie down. Jason then walked around to the driver's side. "Step out of the van, please."

Unsure of what was going on, Noel did as directed.

"I'm going to show you exactly how I feel, okay?" Jason said.

Without waiting for her to answer, he took her in his arms, pulled her close and kissed her. The kiss was long and passionate. It was interrupted by Louie who started barking at their feet. Jason looked Noel in the eye and said, "My feelings for you are only stronger after what I experienced today, and I am more determined than ever to make our relationship work. I've said it before, and I'll say it again. I love you, Noel Summers." He kissed her on both cheeks. "I thank you for sharing your soul with me today."

Without giving Noel a chance to respond, Jason dropped his arms. With Louie at his heels, he walked around to the passenger side of the van. He lifted Louis up onto the seat and was about to climb in himself when he felt a hand on his shoulder. He turned. Noel was right behind him.

"You don't get off that easy without hearing my response," Noel said. She spun Jason around who had a surprised expression on his face. Wrapping her arms around his neck, she pressed her lips to his. Her arms moved down around his waist as she pressed her body into his. "I agree with everything you just said…and you're welcome for today," she said. "And I love you, too."

On the road again, miles passed in silence. They did steal a glance at one another, each occurrence ending with smiles. After a couple more miles, Noel said, "You said you had a couple questions."

"I did," Jason said, trying to remember what else he wanted to ask. When he did, "What was in the boxes we loaded up at the cottage? I noticed they're gone."

"Partially completed quilts. Gabbey sews and likes to make quilts. However, her machine isn't heavy enough to do the actual quilting. My mother has a friend who does, so Gabbey pays her to do it," Noel explained.

"What does she do with the quilts?"

"Some of them are used as winter comforters in the guest rooms. Some are gifts. If Gabbey really likes you, you might get one for Christmas."

Jason laughed. "What a way to tell how someone feels about you."

"It's a gift from the heart," Noel pointed out.

CHAPTER 20

"Haven't seen you around. You've been out all day?" Bobby asked, setting a beer and basket of fish and chips in front of Jason.

Taking a long swallow of beer, Jason set the glass down. "Noel took me to Millbrook."

"The First Nation reservation…her home?" Bobby said with surprise.

"We went to the Culture Center and met her mother."

"Wow!"

"Why do you say that?" Jason asked, pulling the basket of food closer.

Bobby checked the bar to make sure no one needed his attention. "Noel is very friendly and outgoing. However, she keeps her personal life private. She doesn't talk about it much, even with people she trusts. Taking you to Millbrook to meet her mother is telling." Bobby paused to take another survey of the bar. "What did you think?"

"I was honored. The center was amazing, a history book in itself. Her mother was kind and interesting. Have you met her?"

"I've met Noel's mother on numerous occasions. She likes me because I tell her that I'm keeping an eye on her daughter. Although, I'm not sure I've done a very good job of that lately." Bobby paused with a smile. "She's super proud of her children. She's an intelligent woman and understands the changes her culture is going through. Noel's brother and I have been friends for a long time. I try to visit him whenever he's home. I've been up to the casino where he works as well."

Bobby walked away to serve a couple of new customers. When he returned, he continued, "What did Noel's mother think of you?"

"Hard to tell, but Noel gave me the impression she liked me," Jason said.

"Noel has only had two real boyfriends, and she never introduced them to her mother."

"I guess that makes me special," Jason said, a teasing cockiness in his voice.

"Don't let that go to your head, my friend. Noel will see straight through that, as will her mother."

Jason's expression turned serious. "Just kidding. Actually, I was quite honored Noel took me there."

"I hope you realize how lucky you are," Bobby said.

Before Jason could respond that he agreed, Bobby gave him a warning shake of the head. Jason spun around to see Noel coming his way. She was dressed in a blue polo shirt, khaki shorts, and a pair of sandals. He stood and motioned for her to take the seat next to him, which she did. She gave him a kiss on the cheek as she adjusted the bar stool. Looking at Bobby, she said, "I'll just have a water with a lime, please."

Bobby nodded.

"You okay?" Jason asked.

"A little tired," she said as she leaned into him. "It was a long, somewhat emotional day."

Jason responded with, "I understand, my meeting your family and all that." He took a sip of beer. "It all worked out okay, didn't it?"

As Bobby sat the water down, Noel pulled the glass toward her and took a long drink. "I called my girlfriend…you met her. She said my mother spoke very highly of you. She was happy to meet you and hoped you felt the same."

"Very much so," Jason said. "I've been trying to think of a way to thank her for the smudging ceremony."

"You can send her a thank you note. She'd like that," Noel said. "Send it to the Heritage Center. The address is on the brochure you picked up, or you can look it up on the web."

Jason hesitated. "What kind of flowers does your mother like?"

"She likes all kinds, but roses are her favorite."

Jason pulled his phone from his pocket. A short time later, he laid the phone on the bar. "Okay, all done. Actually, I sent them to your mother and staff. I didn't want those girls to get all jealous."

Noel laughed. "Smart thinking. Also, very sweet." She leaned into him further. "My girlfriend also thought you were wonderful."

"Am I?"

"The wind gods have agreed so far."

They sat in silence for a few minutes.

"Thanks again for sharing with me," Jason said.

Noel again kissed him on the cheek. "Tomorrow, you can start practicing again, eh."

Jason glanced over at the instrument that had been covered for several days. "It's the longest time since I started taking lessons seriously that I haven't played."

"I'm sure you'll be fine."

"We'll see," Jason said with a sigh.

CHAPTER 21

Andrew Summers had heard thousands of musicians during his career. He was able to pick up the subtleties of an individual musician with how they played alone and how they merged with others. Thus, he was able to pick up the difference in Jason's playing immediately. Technically, there was no change. Artistically, it was like listening to a totally different pianist. The transformation was amazingly rapid. It was what he had hoped for.

Having finished warming up and playing a few pieces Jason was preparing for his recital, he sat with his hands on his knees, his head bowed, his eyes closed, waiting for his mentor's comments.

Uncle Andy turned the cellphone off he had used to record Jason's play. "I don't think we're going to need this today." Setting the cellphone aside, he continued. "How do you feel, Jason?"

Jason turned toward the man and smiled. "I feel I played well."

"Did you hear any difference?"

Jason hesitated. "Not at first, but as I went along, I felt there was a difference – for the better, I think."

"It evoked heartfelt emotions as well," the maestro suggested.

Jason gave a nod. "I definitely felt more in touch with

the music while I was playing. I felt more relaxed, less tense, just like I've felt since being here in Baddeck." He paused. "I think it's all for the better."

"Your playing has certainly improved," Uncle Andy said. "The transformation in such a short period of time is remarkable. I'd say you've learned to love playing the piano, not just..." Uncle Andy grinned. "What say we leave it at that."

"How did you know that time off would help?" Jason asked.

"I didn't, but I hoped. And it's not just the time off, it's what you did with it. They say a musician plays like he or she lives. I suspect your sole focus up until now has been striving to play perfectly. Now, your focus has changed somewhat, and it shows in your performance. Whatever you're doing to open yourself up, to learn about yourself, is having a positive impact."

"Being here is definitely a different pulse than what I'm used to," Jason acknowledged. "I've enjoyed seeing the country and learning its history and culture."

"This is a beautiful place," Uncle Andy agreed.

"With beautiful, soulful people," Jason said.

Uncle Andy smiled. "Understanding the emotional aspects of music is just as important in a musician's development as mastering the technical side. I suspect, Jason, that in the past you haven't given much thought about yourself, focusing all your energy on your music. You have started that here. I suspect you are becoming as soulful as the Nova Scotians you have met. Continue working on that. You may be surprised what you find."

Jason turned and stared at the piano, his vision becoming blurred. As Uncle Andy said, he had never been a person to delve into his personnel feelings. He had always kept his emotions bottled up, not wanting them to interfere in his music. Here in Baddeck, however, that had changed. The atmosphere around Baddeck and the time away from the piano opened his eyes. The pressure to practice was gone. For the first time, he was able to enjoy and experience other things in harmony with his music, including love. He took a deep breath. Refocusing on Uncle Andy, he said, "Thank you for helping me."

"It's been my pleasure."

Jason rose to his feet and slowly walked around the room. He stopped in front of the curio cabinets, continuing to be in awe at the various awards. Turning to face the maestro, he said, "What happens now?"

"You are beginning to understand the need for balance between your life and your music. Continue to work on that."

"Okay," Jason said. He added quickly, "I have been more spontaneous."

Uncle Andy chuckled. "That's a start." He rose to his feet. "If you have any questions, I'm here."

"Will you be contacting Professor Cunningham?"

"I'll call him later today," Uncle Andy said. "First though, I have a lunch engagement with a wonderful young pianist… who owes me lunch."

• • • • •

They initially kept the conversation light as they sat out on the deck of The Box On The Dock. It was a beautiful, sunny afternoon with the temperature hoovering in the mid-eighties. A breeze coming across the mountains kept the humidity down. The lunch special was a fresh fish sandwich with fries, which each man ordered and declared delicious.

While waiting for cheesecake for dessert, Uncle Andy cleared his throat and asked, "What are your plans once you finish at Barrett?"

It was a question he'd only lately started asking himself. He answered the maestro the same way he answered himself. "I don't have any."

"You haven't thought about it?"

"Yes, sir, I think about it, but I keep telling myself I need to get through the recital first." Jason looked out across Bras d'Or Lake as he continued. "One of the things Dr. Cunningham has stressed over the years is not to get ahead of yourself with the level of difficulty in your music. It can lead to frustration. I think that advice can be expanded to planning ahead for one's future."

"I can understand that and think it's good advice," Uncle Andy said. "However, you only have a few months before graduation."

Jason looked back at the man. "Any suggestions?"

"Do you have an agent?"

Jason's eyes widened. "No. Never thought about that."

Uncle Andy sat back in his chair. "It baffles me that Barrett doesn't teach or guide its students about how to manage their career."

Conversation halted as their cheesecake arrived. When they were finished, Uncle Andy pushed his plate away.

"I'll have my agent call you. His name is William Gregory. His assistant's name is Julia."

"Your agent would take on new graduates?" Jason said, surprised.

"He has other agents who work for him. They even have a new talent section. I'll get him to call you. Anything after that is between you and him."

"Thank you."

"I was in your chair many years ago. If it wasn't for several gray-haired men and a couple women, I wouldn't be sitting on this side of the table. If we ask one thing of those we mentor, it's to always keep an eye out for the next generation."

Jason said, "I would love to have my career be successful enough where I could be a mentor."

"An excellent goal, Jason," Uncle Andy agreed. "An excellent goal."

. . . . .

After Jason paid the check and they were ready to leave, Jason heard a voice that he recognized but could not place. He turned and there was Uncle Henry, captain of *My First Lady III*, talking to a couple of people sitting at a nearby table.

Spotting them, Uncle Henry came over and said, "Jason, Andrew, it's good to see you both. How you doing, Andy? It's been a while."

"I'm doing fine," Uncle Andy said, shaking the captain's hand. "How about yourself?"

"Business is better than I anticipated."

"That's good," Uncle Andy said.

"You still traveling a lot?"

Uncle Andy smiled. "Trying to cut back when I can."

Uncle Henry nodded. "Good seeing you…you, too, Jason. I gotta get down to the boat. A couple tours are coming in this afternoon." He started to walk away and then turned around. "What are you two doing after this?"

"My usual nap after lunch," Uncle Andy said. "Why?"

"I'm short of crew this afternoon. I called Noel and she's going to come along. She's bringing one of the front desk girls who has never been on the boat before. I called Bobby to see if he was interested in bartending. He said he would, but he has his two boys today. I told him to bring them along. They've been on board before and love to drive the boat. So. if you guys want to come along, great. I know you like being out on the lake, Andrew."

Uncle Andy looked at Jason. "It's a beautiful day to be out on the water," he said.

"Then out on the water let's go," Jason said, happy he would be seeing Noel. He didn't mention not knowing Bobby had children.

CHAPTER 22

The late afternoon weather was perfect for a boat ride. The bus tours, having done the Cabot Trail earlier, were anxious to get on board and stretch their legs. The mood was festive. Cindy, the front desk girl, dove right in and helped take drink and snack orders while Bobby worked the bar. Noel took the helm, which let Uncle Henry and First Mate Charlie mingle with the crowd. Charlie was a tall, broad-shouldered man in his late twenties. He was a First Nation Native. Well-built from physical labor, his long black hair was braided down his back. His eyes were black as well, and he had a constant smile.

Charlie did the tour narration while Uncle Henry kept the atmosphere lively with a series of antics and jokes. The two boys who came with Bobby, nine-year-old Freddie and twelve-year-old Allen, stayed with Noel, each biding the time until it was their turn to steer the boat. They were both tall for their ages with long, blond hair. They were polite and well behaved. Uncle Andy stood on the lower stern area watching the scenery pass. Bear and Louie sat at his feet. Jason mingled with the passengers. Everyone was friendly and pleased with the tour so far.

As Jason stopped to get a soda, he noticed Cindy step behind the bar and bump up against Bobby. Both smiled at each other.

Just then, Freddie and Allen came looking for Bobby. "Ms. Noel asked if you could make her a diet soda, please," Allen said. "She also wants us to check on the dogs and make sure they're okay. She hasn't seen them in a while."

"I think they're on the lower deck in the back with Uncle Andy," Jason said. "You guys go look. I'll take Noel her drink."

Jason grabbed the cup of ice and can of soda Bobby set up on the bar and headed toward the helm station. He saw Noel sitting on the captain's chair, looking outward while glancing frequently at the instrument panel. Jason watched her a few moments before she noticed him in the doorway.

"What are you doing?" she asked, accepting the soda can and cup of ice.

"Watching you," Jason replied. He stepped forward and gave her a kiss. "Are Cindy and Bobby a couple?"

"They started going out shortly after Cindy arrived this summer," Noel said.

"That's nice," Jason said. "What about Bobby's boys, Freddie and Allen?"

"Oh, he's not their father," Noel explained. "Their mother is one of the housekeeping supervisors at the cottage. She works hard to take care of those boys. Bobby has been involved with them for a few years and takes them occasionally on his day off. They've been out on the boat before and love the water." Noel paused. "Don't ask their mother about their father. All she will say is that he's not in the picture and never will be."

"That's unfortunate," Jason said.

"That's one of the reasons Bobby does what he can."

Jason again hesitated with his next question. Finally, "What does Cindy think about them?"

"Oh, she loves them to death." Noel let out a laugh. "And don't let Cindy's bubbling personality fool you. Bobby told me she gives them very little room to wiggle." Noel took a long drink of her soda. "You want to drive some?"

"Sure?"

They switched positions with a quick kiss. Noel turned off the autopilot so Jason could practice steering the boat.

"By the way," Noel said, emptying the rest of her soda into her cup. She offered it to Jason who took a drink. "Gabbey was asking if your suite was okay and whether you had any complaints."

Jason gave a shrug. "The room is great," he said. "Gabbey even put some plants in the room. The staff is wonderful as well."

Noel reached over and gave him a shoulder rub. "I'll let Gabbey know you're okay with everything."

Jason snickered. "Well, I do have one small issue." Noel's eyes widened slightly. Jason continued. "I don't get any of those little shampoo bottles or cakes of soap."

The shoulder rub changed to a shoulder smack. Before Jason could respond, they were interrupted by the stampede of two dogs followed by two young boys piling into the pilot house. "We're back," Freddy announced.

Noel first directed her attention to the dogs, getting them to settle down beneath the helm seat. Looking at the two boys, she said, "What have you guys been up to?"

"Mingling with the guests," Allen said, sounding adult-like.

"Can we steer?" Freddie interrupted, stepping up beside

Jason. Jason looked at Noel who nodded her head. Jason stepped out of the way so Freddie could take over.

"I'll stay with them if you want to walk around some more," Noel said. "Maybe you can grab some snacks on your way back."

Jason blew Noel a kiss as he exited the pilot house. He stopped and spoke to Bobby while watching Cindy scurry around taking drink orders. Uncle Henry and Charlie were moving from table to table, pointing out areas of interest along the shores. Uncle Henry kept the crowd laughing as he mixed an array of jokes in with the narration.

. . . . .

Jason found Uncle Andy standing on the back deck looking over the stern rail. The engines plus the background noise of the people inside kept him from noticing Jason at first. The man stood taking in the scenery, seemingly lost in his own thoughts. Jason wondered what went through the mind of a man such as Andrew Summers with his immense talent. *Such a career, yet so down to earth. An amazing man,* Jason thought.

A few days earlier, when Jason looked up Andrew Summers online, he'd found, besides the expected impressive body of work, an interview on YouTube, mostly Andy talking about how and why he worked in so many musical styles. But there was something else, too…something missing. Jason had buried the thought, figuring if the opportunity ever presented itself, he'd ask.

Uncle Andy finally sensed Jason's presence. He turned and smiled. "A beautiful afternoon for a boat ride, isn't it?" he said.

"Yes, it is," Jason returned. "Although I imagine every day is a beautiful day out here on this lake."

"I agree," Uncle Andy said.

"Mind if I join you?" Jason said, hesitating to move further through the doorway

"Please do."

Pointing to Uncle Andy's near-empty glass of wine, Jason said, "Need a refill?"

The maestro raised the glass. "Not yet, maybe in a few."

Jason moved to stand beside the man. They stood side by side for a moment before Uncle Andy turned in Jason's direction. "I hope you've enjoyed our time together, and I hoped you feel I've helped you."

Jason looked toward the man. "You have been very helpful in ways I could never have imagined. I didn't know what to expect when Professor Cunningham sent me up here. I certainly didn't expect to meet you, or for you to help me the way you have. I want you to know I will always be grateful for that."

"Those are very kind words, thank you." The maestro took a sip of his wine. "As I said before, I am open to any questions you may have."

"I don't have any questions about me. I do have a question about you, though." Jason ventured.

"Alright."

"Your repertoire of work is very eclectic. I've watched

some of the interviews you have given and understand why." Jason hesitated as he debated whether to ask the question he'd been thinking about after his internet search. He decided to go ahead, although it didn't come out as an actual question. "Focusing on your classical compositions, you have only written symphonies or music for groups of instruments." Another short pause. "You have never written a concerto, something featuring only one instrument."

"Very insightful," Uncle Andy said. He emptied his glass of wine. "Know this though, most artists, regardless of the genre, produce more work than the public ever sees."

"You mean you have…"

Jason didn't finish the sentence as the sound of the diesels changed. "Looks like we're getting ready to dock," Uncle Andy said. "Don't know that I can be much help, but I'm going to at least offer." He held his glass toward Jason. "I'll take that refill now."

Jason took the glass and watched Uncle Andy walk away.

CHAPTER 23

That evening, Jason sat on the veranda enjoying a chicken Caesar salad and sipping a freshly-brewed iced tea. He took his time eating, which was new for him. In the past, he was always on a tight schedule, and thus eating was often rushed. Since arriving in Baddeck, he'd had no schedule. His eyes had been opened to life outside of his music. He was learning to relax, to slow down. His heart had been opened to love. And it all showed in his piano playing. Uncle Andy thought the transformation was astonishing. It would be several weeks before Dr. Cunningham could give his assessment. Jason was hopeful that it would be positive as well.

As he finished his meal, Gabbey walked up and sat down across from him. "How was your salad?"

"Excellent," Jason responded. "The chicken was fantastic. I'll go back to the kitchen later and give Cookie a shout," Jason said.

"He'll like that," Gabbey said. She looked out towards the town. The forecasted rain looked imminent with signs in the distance that it was coming over the mountain. "We have a lot of guests running around in town tonight. I hope they get back before the storm hits," she said, nodding in that direction. "Anyway, I came out to ask if you were going to play tonight. We expect a good crowd, even bigger if it rains. Tips should be good."

Jason smiled. He didn't remind her that he didn't keep the tips, instead distributing them among the staff. Still, it would be good for them.

"I want to call my sister and take a shower, then I'll be back down. Is that okay?"

"Works for me. Tell your sister I said hello."

"I will."

Gabbey rose from her seat and walked back toward the dining room. Jason watched as she stopped briefly at each occupied table. Jason observed that not only was Gabbey excellent at her job, she seemed to thoroughly enjoy it.

Jason thought about that idea for a moment. He let out a slow breath. While he still had to work hard and stay focused, he was learning the importance of having a balance in his life. Did he think he could find joy in his life and in his music? Before coming to Baddeck, he would not have been able to give an answer. Now, the answer was yes.

. . . . .

Jason was about to disconnect the call when his sister finally picked up, saying, "Jason, how are you? Haven't heard from you in a while."

"I'm great, Laura. How about you?"

"Same, 'ole, same 'ole," Laura said. "Business is good. Mom's getting ready for the fall shows. I'm doing what I can to help."

"You two make a great team," Jason said.

"I think so," Laura responded. "Anyway, what have you been up to?"

"Learning about myself and getting to know the area. I've been doing some touristy things. It's really beautiful here."

"Are you having fun?"

"More than fun," Jason spouted without thinking. As soon as he said it, he knew it was a mistake.

However, his sister made no comment. Instead, "So, you're using your time well?"

"I think so. Learning to balance my life out some."

"How's the recital prep going?"

"Okay. I'm going downstairs to play in the bar when we're finished."

"You're playing in a *bar*!?"

"They have a piano in the lounge. I practice there."

"Oh," Laura said. "Have you met this Uncle Andy guy Professor Cunningham sent you to see?" she added curiously.

"Yes, I've met him," Jason said. "You'd be surprised to learn who Uncle Andy is," Jason chuckled. "Ever hear the name Andrew Summers?"

Laura paused. "I've heard of Andrew Summers, the composer, yes."

"That's Uncle Andy."

"You're kidding me?"

"Nope." Jason spent time explaining the rest of the story.

"Wait til I tell Mom and Dad. They won't believe me."

"Then they'll just have to come up here and see for themselves," Jason said. "You guys will love this place. It's full of history and wonderful people. The scenery is unbelievable. It might even stimulate you to design a new line of clothing."

"Dad probably wouldn't like it. Too desolate. He wouldn't be able to work," Laura said.

"Actually, the Internet service is surprisingly good. Tourists don't want to be out of contact with the real world," Jason explained.

Laura paused briefly. "So tell me about *her.*"

"About who?"

"I doubt *More Than Fun* is her name."

Jason shook his head side to side. He should have known better than to think he could get anything past his sister. "Her name is Noel Summers."

"Same last name as Andrew Summers," Laura pointed out.

"They're related somehow through marriage," Jason said. He let out a chuckle. "Then again, everybody here is related somehow or another."

"Tell me about her," Laura pressed.

"She works here at the cottage and is studying hotel/restaurant management. She's very bright... and very beautiful."

"Oh, my," Laura moaned. "Cunningham sent you up there to improve your playing and instead you fall in love. And don't deny it. I can hear it in your voice."

Jason let out a slow breath. "Taking time off and meeting Noel has helped my performance tremendously. I'm more relaxed, which allows me to better feel the music. I have a way to go, but my playing certainly has improved.

"Anyway," Jason continued. "Talk to Mom and Dad about coming up for a visit."

"Will do," Laura said. "And Jason...I'm happy for you."

"Thank you. That means a lot," Jason said.

"Love you."

"Love you, too."

. . . . .

There was quite a crowd at the cottage, as Gabbey had predicted. The rain did keep many from wandering into town, dining instead at the cottage and staying around for the after-dinner activities. Rumor had it a guest was going to play the piano later.

When Jason walked in a little before 7:30, the dining room and lounge area were filled to near capacity. He went to the far end of the bar where there was one seat left. Sliding onto the stool, he waved to Bobby, who waved back. There were two other bartenders working as well. When one came up to him, he ordered iced tea with lemon. Jason felt a little nervous about playing tonight. He didn't know if it was because of the time off or because it had been a while since he had played in front of such a large audience. Previous crowds at the cottage had been a quarter of this size or less. He took a deep breath, telling himself to relax and enjoy himself.

He picked up his iced tea, dropped some money on the bar, and headed toward the piano. He pulled the cover off gently, folding and setting it aside. He placed his drink on a small table next to the piano, sat down and closed his eyes a few moments. Then he began to play. A few easy warm-up scales followed by more complicated exercises. He added his own flair to the exercises, to the point where some in the audience thought he was actually playing a classical piece. Warmed up, he started playing portions of a few classical pieces, focusing on Beethoven and Chopin. Then he started going through other pieces he was considering for the recital.

He played continuously for an hour, occasionally smiling at the crowd. Otherwise, he was oblivious to everything going on around him. He felt one with the music. When he finished the last piece, Chopin's Nocturne No.2, he closed his eyes and bowed his head. Flexing his fingers, he took a couple deep breaths. When he opened his eyes and looked across the room, he saw that most of the crowd were on their feet applauding. He rose to his feet, a little embarrassed at the attention, and bowed. When he had played here before, the crowd had always been appreciative, but never like this. He smiled and waved.

"Thank you…thank you," he said. More applause followed. When it died down, he said, "If anybody has any requests, let me know, I'll do my best."

A couple song titles were called out. He set his iPad on the music stand and looked for the titles. A few minutes later, he was playing them. After both pieces were completed, he received another hefty round of applause. The tip jar that Bobby had set up on the bar was filling rapidly.

. . . . .

For the next hour, Jason mixed in requests with pieces he needed to practice. The tables in the dining room turned over with other guests. However, many migrated to the lounge area, keeping Bobby and the other two bartenders busy. Gabbey ventured over and listened a few minutes from the sidelines. She picked up the change in Jason's playing. He had always played exceptionally well. Tonight, he was playing beautifully.

Noel came over as well. When Jason finished a piece and the applause started, she looked at Gabbey and said, "What a crowd!"

Gabbey simply nodded and walked away. A minute later, she was in her office making a phone call. When the person answered, she said without saying hello, "You'd better get over here and see what you've created!"

. . . . .

Uncle Andy walked into the lounge area thirty minutes later. He was pleasantly surprised at the size of the crowd and quickly understood why as he heard Jason playing. He made his way to the far end of the bar, saying hi to a few locals, smiling at the tourists who looked at him as if they might know him but couldn't place his face. He had his hair in a ponytail which is not how he wore it when he was on stage. He was wearing a polo shirt and khaki slacks. An old pair of boat shoes covered his sockless feet.

Bobby came up to him as he settled in his seat. "What can I get you?" the bartender asked as he shook the man's hand.

"Any new local brews?"

"We have a light summer ale that's getting good reviews."

"Sounds good," Uncle Andy said. He turned towards the piano. He closed his eyes to better focus on Jason's playing of

Beethoven's First Piano Concerto. Uncle Andy knew it was one of the pieces Jason was preparing for the recital.

"I guess our little town has helped you, Mr. Kinde," the maestro said under his breath. "Having an audience helps, also."

He took a swallow of the beer Bobby placed before him. Nodding his approval, he returned his attention to Jason. He listened as Jason continued to mix pieces he was preparing for his recital with requests, mostly standard tunes. Each piece was played exquisitely. The speed of Jason's transformation continued to amaze Andrew Summers. In addition, Jason seemed to be enjoying himself as he was smiling and interacting with the crowd.

The music continued. The crowd was appreciative. Uncle Andy sat back and watched. After finishing his second beer, he dropped some money on the bar. He looked at his watch as he slid off the barstool. "Not too late to make a phone call," he said. He let out a soft chuckle. "Cunningham isn't going to believe a word I say."

He stopped at the couple steps leading to the lobby. Turning for one more look at Jason as thought crossed his mind. "Maybe…just maybe, he's the one," the maestro mouthed silently.

CHAPTER 24

Jason closed and locked the door. He kicked off his shoes and fell across the bed. It had been a tiring day, both physically and emotionally, ending with the three and a half hours he played at the bar. The evening finished with nearly two hundred dollars in his tip bucket. He assumed that was a good amount. Bobby certainly thought so as Jason insisted the bartender distribute the money among the staff.

Jason was pleased with his playing, both technically and artistically, though he'd also noticed places in both areas where he could improve. The crowd certainly seemed appreciative of what and how he'd played. He had no doubt coming to Baddeck was worth it. Now, he had to continue taking advantage of the opportunity.

A knocking on his door broke his train of thought. Jumping up, he looked through the peephole, breaking into a smile as he opened the door. Noel stood there, still dressed in her uniform of the day. Her hair was somewhat disheveled, but she still looked beautiful.

"Hi, gorgeous," he said, the earlier fatigue fading as he ushered her in.

"Hi," Noel returned, stepping through the doorway.

. . . . .

Noel moved into the room, taking a quick glance around. There was nothing to comment about as Jason was a super neat person. Turning in a circle, she said, "It's been a long time since I've been in this suite, or any of the rooms in this wing. We reserve this area for special and long-term guests, and you're the first long-termer we've had in a while."

"It's nice. Plus, it's quiet," Jason said.

"Anyway." She turned to face him and held out a small gift bag she had brought with her. "I brought you a present."

His earlier smile widened as he took the bag and lifted out a small bottle of shampoo and a couple small cakes of soap.

"Well, thank you…thank you very much." He set the bag on a side table. "How was your day?"

"Tiring," Noel said. She leaned against the doorway leading to the bedroom. "We had our best evening so far this season, largely because of you."

"I'm sure the weather played a part." He pointed to the gift bag. "Anyway, thanks again."

"You're welcome." Noel turned to leave.

"You have to go?"

Noel shrugged. "I suspect you're tired."

"Not that tired." He stepped toward her, wrapping her in his arms and pushing her backwards. They fell side by side onto the closest bed. Noel rolled on top of him, her hands on his chest. She leaned forward and kissed him passionately. Jason's hands slid down her back to her bottom. He gave her a gentle squeeze, causing her to press into him. Their lips parted as she let out a soft moan. She pushed to an upright position. Reaching down she pulled her shirt up over her head. Tossing it aside, she reached back and unclipped her bra. She tossed that aside as well. She leaned into him, a breast pressing against his lips. "Kiss me like you did before," she said softly.

They undressed one another slowly, carefully, passionately. Sounds of pleasure and passion followed. They started slowly, kissing, caressing, each savoring the sensations shooting through their bodies. Jason pulled her tighter to him. She responded with increased motion. Noel's hair broke loose and fell across her chest. He reached up and pushed it away, caressing her as he did. She let him know her feelings with a passionate kiss.

Their movements became faster and more synchronized. "Wait for me," she whispered through her teeth. "Wait for me."

They came together a short time later.

Noel collapsed on top of Jason. He held her tightly. He pressed into her, she into him. Their hearts beat against one another. They struggled to control their breathing. Finally, Noel slid to the side. They kissed. They kissed again. Jason had trouble keeping his hands off of her, his fingers seeking and finding her most sensitive areas. She did the same.

Jason adjusted his position so he could kiss her breasts, at the same time reaching down to touch her.

She reached down and grabbed him. "You can't be ready again!"

He responded with a soft moan.

Her free hand holding his head against her chest, Noel

rolled onto her back. She guided him into her. They started moving as one.

"Oh my God," she nearly bellowed.

. . . . .

Jason rolled onto his elbow as he looked Noel in the eyes. He moved her hair from her face. Wiping a bead of sweat from her forehead, he said, "I thought earlier it had been a wonderful day. Now, I don't have words powerful enough to describe it."

Noel kissed him lightly on the lips. "Then don't try. Our memories will be enough," she said.

"I love you."

"And I love you."

Jason kissed her. "I want you in my life and at my side."

She pressed his hand firmly against her chest. "What do we do in the meantime…until we know the future, that is?"

Jason pulled his hand away, covering the area with his lips. "We could continue where we just left off."

"Jason, I need to work tomorrow."

Jason pulled away and sat up on the edge of the bed. He picked up the gift bag sitting on the bedside table. "Or we could go take a shower."

He started to rise, but Noel grabbed his arm. He turned and looked at Noel who was lying on her back. She pulled him on top of her as she said, "I just remembered, I'm off tomorrow. What say we take that shower later?"

. . . . .

It was close to midnight as Uncle Andy walked slowly through the streets of Baddeck, as he had been doing for the past couple of hours. The sky was clear. The moon and a few streetlamps together gave enough light to make walking along the uneven pavement relatively safe. He had nowhere to go except home to his bed. He had nothing planned for the next several days, just as he liked it.

In his younger days, Andrew Summers lived for the chaos of his career. Traveling was something he looked forward to, especially when his wife went with him. Since her death, he'd sold their apartments in New York and Boston. His only home now was here in Baddeck. While he still loved the actual making of music, the travel requirements were becoming more and more tiring. When he was away, he found himself longing for his own bed, his own town, the lake, the surrounding mountains, and the people. He often thought he'd work with students from the Lunenburg Academy. He had visited the beautiful town of Lunenburg and the music academy numerous times, always incognito as Uncle Andy, never wanting to be more than a tourist. However, Lunenburg was not an easy commute from Baddeck.

He looked out toward the lake. The lake's surface was brightly lit from the moonlight. There were a few faint lights visible from the far shore. He stopped walking and closed his eyes a moment, imagining what it would look like on a bright sunny day. The image then turned to a snow-covered scene. He'd always had a vivid imagination, a necessity for a composer of not only classical music but music scores and movie soundtracks as well. Tonight was no different.

As he walked, he thought about the young man, Jason Kinde, sitting at the piano in the Baddeck Cottage lounge. Tonight, the young man's playing was effortless. The sounds were melodic and pleasing to the ear. The maestro's thoughts returned to earlier in the day when Jason asked about his own repertoire of compositions, specifically the lack of a concerto. The maestro had responded that not all music written was published. An earlier idea continued to scroll through his mind as he walked. Uncle Andy's imagination kicked in as he saw Jason at the piano center stage, a full orchestra in the background. Andrew Summers, himself, conducting.

The scene was interrupted as a gust of wind came down the street. Uncle Andy turned and took another look across the town, across the lake. "Are you the one, Jason Kinde?" he said into the night air. "Are you the one?" He paused as another gust of wind messaged his face. "I believe you just might be."

CHAPTER 25

Jason awoke slowly. He reached across the bed, but it was empty. He sat up and threw his legs over the side. There was a note on the bedside table. A smile formed. The note was simple and to the point. *Good morning. Meet me at the pool at 9:00 am. We'll work out together. N.*

Five minutes later, Jason was out the door. The chlorinated humidity struck him as he entered the pool area. Noel was already in the water. She wore a dark blue one-piece bathing suit. He watched her as she made it to the far end of the pool, dove under the water and pushed off against the wall for a return lap. He walked to the end of the pool where she would make the next turn. Her strokes were powerful yet graceful. As she approached the end, she noticed him. She reached up and grabbed the edge.

Looking up with a smile, she said, "Come on in, the water's perfect."

Not wanting to delay getting into the water, Jason dropped his towel. He slipped out of his sandals and tee shirt. As he already knew the water was deep enough at this end, he dove over her, entering the water about as ungracefully as possible.

Noel laughed as he came up sputtering water. Swimming toward her, Jason wrapped his arms around her and gave her a good morning kiss.

"How long have you been here?" Jason asked.

She looked at the waterproof watch she wore when she swam. "About forty minutes."

"You're not even short of breath!"

Jason leaned in for another kiss. Pushing him away gently, Noel added, "Behave. There're a couple guests in the gym. Come on, do some laps with me." She skirted around him and headed across the pool. Jason let her get a couple lengths ahead before taking off after her.

They swam steadily for another thirty minutes; or rather Noel swam steadily, Jason swam a lap and held on to the edge for a few seconds to catch his breath. Swimming as a cardio workout was much different than his workouts in the gym or running in the park.

When she was finished, Noel waited on the edge for Jason to catch up. Noel pushed a strand of hair off his face as she said, "What are your plans for the day?"

"You're off, right?" Jason said.

"Yes," Noel replied. "I was going to suggest we go to breakfast somewhere and then go on a hike. Supposed to be hot today, but no rain. There's a lot of options on the Cabot Trail, but I have one I think you'll like."

"Sounds like a plan."

They parted as they exited the pool building with plans to meet by Noel's Jeep in forty-five minutes. Noel told Jason to dress for the hike as they would leave right from wherever they ate.

Jason took the stairs and hurried down the hall to his room. Housekeeping had already been in. Bed and bath linens had been changed, and the room had been cleaned. Evidence of the previous night's activities had vanished. Which was fine, except they weren't due to clean his room for a couple more days. *How did...* Jason stopped the thought short. He didn't want to know the answer.

. . . . .

As they loaded up the Jeep, Noel asked Jason if he could wait a half an hour or so to eat, saying they could get breakfast at a tourist shop at the base of the trail she wanted to go on.

"She makes the best egg-and-sausage biscuits," Noel said. "She also makes homemade doggy treats." She looked at the dogs who were getting settled in the back. "Isn't that right, guys?" On cue, both dogs barked.

Thirty minutes later, they were parked outside of a wide, one-story, metal-framed building. The spacious parking lot was half-full. It was a popular spot, as the view out over the area was spectacular. The store was dog-friendly, so Bear and Louie were let out as soon as the Jeep's door was open. The animals stopped in front of the vehicle for a moment to get their bearings and then tore off around the side. "Sally, the owner, knows the dogs," Noel explained. "She'll let them in the back and give them their treats."

The store was all geared toward the tourist, including an area stocked with hiking supplies, which Jason surveyed. He next turned his attention to the large trail map pinned to the wall.

Noel came up behind him, giving his shoulder a gentle

rub. “Don’t worry, we’re not going on any of those, ours is more difficult.” Noel pointed to an area behind the store that showed no markings. “There’s a trail straight up the mountain hidden in the undergrowth. It’s not for public use,” Noel said. “It leads to the fire watch tower at the top of the mountain. It’s run by the park service. Most of the colleges in the maritime area have a forestry program. The park service hires these students for the summer. They get paid and get college credits.”

“Why are we going there?” Jason said, trepidation in his voice.

“I help with supplies. We’ll take a load up today,” Noel said. “Plus, I want to get the tower aired out and make sure everything is in working order. If there’s anything to do, Alex or one of his crew will come up and fix it.” Before Jason could make a comment concerning his ability to do the same, Noel continued. “Don’t worry, I don’t expect you to carry anything. It’s a steep trek up the hill.”

“I’ll carry whatever I can,” Jason insisted.

They continued strolling around the store, Jason picking up a couple souvenirs to take home. They eventually made their way to the food counter, where they ordered breakfast sandwiches to go. Just then an elderly lady came out from the back with a tray of sandwiches. Seeing Noel, she handed the tray off to one of the counter girls and came around to give her a hug.

“You could have called to let me know you were coming,” the woman scolded, kiddingly. “I wouldn’t have been so surprised to see your dogs in the back.”

On cue as always, Bear and Louise came traipsing around the corner, each with a treat in their mouth. The woman laughed and gave the animals a head rub. She was a short, stocky, dark-haired woman who looked like she had lived in the wilderness her entire life.

Noel introduced the woman as Sally, the store's proprietor. They chatted for a few minutes. Sally didn't have to ask about Jason as the look from Noel gave the story. Noel asked Jason to get the breakfast order while she took care of the dogs and looked at the supplies Sally was putting together for the tower. While Sally wasn't the sole provider of supplies, she was one of the major contributors contracted by the park service.

Sally already had several backpacks loaded. They were lined up against the wall in the order she thought they should be delivered. Sally told Jason each weighted around forty pounds.

Grabbing the first pack in line, Jason said, "I think I can handle one of these."

Noel handed Jason a large fanny pack as well. "Strap this to the top of the backpack. This is water and energy bars for us."

Noel helped Jason put the backpack on so it was balanced and the straps were tight. He insisted it felt okay. She reinforced that if he had a problem not to worry. There were waterproof drop boxes placed along the trail.

Noel told Jason that she loved serving as a trail guide for the various trails in the area. However, she also enjoyed the solitude of hiking alone with the dogs, or like now, with him and the dogs. "I'll have to keep a close eye on everyone's stamina," she said, "including my own, as this is the first trip to the tower this season."

Sally had made doggy saddle bags for the volunteers with large-breed dogs. They couldn't carry much, but every couple bottles of water helped. Louie got a smaller bag that contained a few doggie treats. Bear came running around the side with the saddle bag strapped to his back. There was a bottle of water in each pocket. He wasn't fazed by the extra weight as he had made several similar trips up the mountain over the years. Louie followed Bear with his own doggie bag, happy to be participating in the adventure.

Sally reminded Noel to call down on the radio when they arrived. Sally had the radio in the store on constantly during the fire season and whenever there were people going up the trail.

As Noel, Jason and the dogs entered the tree line where the actual trail began, the incline gradually increased. Louis and Bear ran ahead while Noel set a slower pace. There was plenty of sunlight filtering through the trees without it beating directly down on them. The temperature was much cooler than in town, yet the humidity remained high. The trail was worn from use over the years, however, snow had loosened up the soil and caused a few small rockslides. Noel cautioned Jason to keep a close eye on the terrain so as not to slip and or twist an ankle.

Jason quickly put any discomfort or concerns away as he was engulfed by the surrounding noise and foliage. He heard a variety of birds, including a woodpecker working on its new home. Rustling leaves caused by the breeze and unseen animals added to the atmosphere's symphony. Except to make a comment about the degree of incline continuing to rise, he said nothing until they took a break at the thirty-minute mark. They each drank a half bottle of water and ate the breakfast sandwiches they'd carried with them.

"Remember we talked about supply priorities?" Noel said. "Hydration is the number one concern for hikers. It will be even more so as the weather gets hotter. That's why we start bringing water up first." She poured some of her water into a couple bowls for the dogs, who lapped it up hurriedly.

"There's no water on this side of the mountain, but there are a couple streams near the top on the other side," Noel explained. "One is from an underground spring and is always cold and refreshing. While it's been dependable since I've been involved, we still stock the tower with jugs of water."

Jason took another swallow of water. He picked up his backpack and started after the dogs, who were already on the move.

. . . . .

Noel watched Jason a few moments before lifting her own backpack. Earlier thoughts she had about him scrolled through her mind. She had pegged him as a city boy when he first arrived. While he may have been that, he certainly was adjusting well. There were other things about Jason Kinde that were amazing as well. She had never heard anyone play the piano live like him, and he was still in school. He had come to Baddeck to work on his artistry, as he called it. A short time with Uncle Andy, and that had improved.

And then there was Jason, the….

Noel cut the thoughts off, telling herself not to get distracted as they had a steep climb ahead of them. *Symbolic,* she thought. She tightened the straps on her backpack and headed after Jason and the dogs.

• • • • •

Thankfully, the trip up to the tower was uneventful. Jason continued to be in awe of the surroundings. It was a beautiful time of the year as the spring flowers were just starting to bloom and the trees were starting to fill, yet you could still see deep into the woods. Noel told him that spring was her favorite time in the mountains.

When they reached the clearing where the tower stood, Noel told Jason to set his pack down and take a breather. She would climb the hundred plus steps up to the top and open everything up.

"They rigged a pulley system a couple years ago to haul the supplies up," Noel explained. "Put your load over there by the shed." She pointed to the left where there was a storage shed built from what looked like leftover pieces of lumber. Next to that was an old-fashioned outhouse.

"No plumbing or cable TV?" Jason joked, putting his backpack down and sitting on a tree stump. He pulled a bottle of water from his fanny pack and offered it to Noel, which she accepted. He then filled two water bowls for the dogs, which they lapped right down.

He took the opportunity to examine the tower more

closely. He guessed it was at least a hundred feet tall. Noel was already a quarter of the way up. He watched as she took each step followed by a very brief pause and then the next. It was as if she was climbing the steep slope of a mountain, which in a way she was. It seemed much quicker than expected when Jason heard a thump at the base of the steps. He looked up and saw Noel leaning over the rail. She was motioning that he should put the backpacks in the basket she had lowered and come on up himself. She had told him on the way up the trail that the dogs would stay below.

Making sure the backpacks were secure in the basket, Jason watched them start to rise. He then began his own ascent skyward. When he reached the top, his legs burned from lactic buildup. He stood on the outside deck, bent forward, his hands on his knees. Noel had warned him about the altitude change. That hadn't been a major problem coming up the mountain trail. Now, however, it seemed to be hitting him hard.

Handing him a bottle of water, Noel said, "Nothing about hiking in the mountains is a rush unless you're being chased by a bear or running away from a fire. Everything else is a planned, controlled motion."

"I thought you weren't supposed to run from bears," Jason said, twisting open the water bottle.

Noel laughed. "Depends on how hungry they look."

Jason laughed. He straightened up, worked a kink out of his back, and took a couple deep breaths. "Everything okay up here?"

"A couple of the storm shutters are loose," Noel said.

"Otherwise, I don't see any damage from the winter." She pointed to the radio sitting on a table against the far wall. "I called Sally to let her know we're here. She asked how you made out. I told her you did fine. Go ahead and take a look around. I'm going to tighten the screws on the shutters hinges."

The tower offered a spectacular three-hundred-and-sixty-degree view of the mountain range. The floor was wooden planks set tightly together. The surface was smooth and worn. The ceiling was the rafters holding the roof. There were tables set about with lamps, some oil, some battery-operated. A camping stove and kitchen utensils also sat on one table. Noel explained that because the generator fuel had to carried up the mountain, the generator was used sparingly.

Wall decorations consisted of area photographs and framed lists of policies and procedures, including the emergency evacuation process. One wall held photographs of the summer crews over the years. The rest of the interior looked well planned and well organized. Jason did notice that there were no bedrooms. Cots lined the walls, sitting low to the floor, so that whoever was on watch could see out.

"How do you wash dishes?" Jason asked.

"Minimize them, for one. Use the cans the product comes in or one pot dishes. Fresh fruits and veggies, although heavy to transport, are a big part of their diet as well. Those don't have to be cooked. They are taught to plan their meals with all this in mind but also to stay well-nourished and have enough variety not to get bored." Noel pointed to a near-empty jar sitting on a table. "They also go through a lot of bread and peanut butter."

While Noel continued her inspection and minor repair duties, Jason ventured outside. Holding onto the rail, he made his way around the deck that circled the entire structure. He gazed out over the mountains, continuing to be mesmerized by the beauty before him. His walk around the outside completed, he helped Noel with the shutters.

"So how does this work, I mean with people watching out for fires?" he asked.

"There's always at least three people here, four makes it much easier. They work scheduled watches. The person or persons not on a watch attend to basic chores. What time they have left, and there is usually a significant amount of free time, they can do whatever they want, including getting ahead on their schoolwork. They are encouraged to get plenty of exercise and rest."

"What happens if they see smoke?" Jason asked.

Noel explained. "If they see something suspicious, they have a large scope that can set up on one of the braces you see along the rails. This also gives them direction and distance. They do their best to locate the source. Once they have that information, they call it in right away. Then they keep a close eye on it."

"If it's close to the tower?"

"They evacuate. Safety always comes first."

"What about people who are out on the trail already, like you might be out with a tour?"

"Tour guides always carry radios," Noel explained. "If the fire risk is too high, we don't go."

They finished in the tower and stowed away the supplies

they had carried up the hill. Noel was satisfied everything was in working order and there was no need for Alex or his crew to come up until the tower was manned. While not in a hurry, she told Jason she wanted to enjoy the trek down the mountain. "There are a couple side trails we can explore if we have time," she said. "I like hiking through areas seldom used."

"Not part of your tourist trails, eh?" Jason said.

"This tower trail is off limits anyway," Noel reminded. "But there are other side trails we locals like to keep to ourselves."

Closing the windows, they took one more walk around the perimeter. As Noel locked the door, Jason was right behind her, his arms circling her waist. Before she could say anything, his lips covered hers. The kiss was passionate and long. They kissed again. She started to say something when she heard the dogs barking down below.

"Jason, I'd love to stay here, but Bear and Louie have other ideas."

Jason gave her another quick kiss. "I understand," he said. "Maybe we can bring another load of supplies up soon."

Noel laughed as she stepped away. "Let's get down and see what the dogs are howling about."

CHAPTER 26

When they returned to the cottage, Jason bid goodbye to Noel and the two dogs. He headed to his room for a nap, with plans to meet Noel at the pool before dinner for a swim.

"It will help minimize the stiffness tomorrow morning," she insisted.

"Sounds good to me," Jason agreed.

Jason walked through the lobby, wanting to check for any mail. There was none, and he was about to step away when Cindy called to him.

"Wait a second, Jason, there is a package for you." She pulled a large manila envelope from beneath the counter. "I almost forgot about this, sorry. This was left before I got here this morning."

It was thick and heavy with Jason's name handwritten across the front. It was sealed with shipping tape. There were no post office or delivery company marks. Jason thanked her. In his room a few minutes later, he opened the package and slid the contents out. There was a group of papers in a manila folder. Atop of that were two sheets of paper folded in half. He unfolded the papers and began to read.

Dear Mr. Kinde,

I believe your time here in Baddeck has been beneficial for you as a person and as a musician. I can certainly attest to the latter. The key now as you move forward in your career is to live these lessons learned. I have confidence that you have the talent and willpower to do just that. Stay true to yourself and listen to the advice of those around you, and I feel success will follow.

The last time we were together, you asked about my lack of compositions for individual instruments. I explained that not all of a composer's work is published. I can attest to that. I have enclosed one of my unpublished compositions, a concerto for piano and orchestra in G minor. It is untitled and has never been performed. Until now, I have not found anyone I could trust to interpret the piece in a fashion I believe it deserves. I have now found that person. That person is you.

The work is in three movements. Technically, it is difficult, but I believe within your capability. The key, and what has held me back until now, is the ability to interpret the music. When I first heard you play, I didn't even think about this piece for you. However, after your remarkable improvement and hearing you play last night, I believe you may be the one.

Enclosed is a copy of the score in its entirety.

A couple legal points before I close. This is a copyrighted work and is being given to you for your study. You have my permission to perform the work in public, as long as there is no monetary remuneration. We can discuss those issues when and if that time comes, which I certainly hope occurs. The exception is the tips you earn playing at the Baddeck Cottage.

After you have had an opportunity to analyze and practice the work, I will make myself available to discuss any questions or concerns. I eagerly await this conversation.

Your Box On The Dock lunch partner,

Uncle Andy

Jason read the letter three times. He finally set it aside and picked up the concerto and began thumbing through the pages. Thirty minutes later, he stared at the papers in his lap. Not only did he feel tremendously honored at the gesture, he also felt an enormous weight on his shoulders to act appropriately, responsibly.

He picked up the score and headed for the door. He pulled out his cell phone and dialed Noel's number.

She answered on the third ring, sounding like she had been awoken from her nap.

Jason apologized for this but quickly added, "Can you come down to the lounge?"

Concern replaced the fatigue in her voice. "What's the matter, Jason?"

Sensing this, Jason continued, "Nothing's wrong. I just want you to come down ...please."

Noel said, "Okay. Give me a few minutes."

. . . . .

After taking a quick shower, Noel pulled on a pair of shorts and a red uniform polo shirt. She tried to surmise what could be so important that Jason wanted her down in the lounge right away. As she couldn't come up with anything, she told herself to be patient.

"So much for a swim," she said, heading out the door.

She went in through the lobby where she found Cindy at the front desk. She gave the girl a *what's up* look. The front desk clerk gave her the I *have no clue what you're talking about* look in return. Noel didn't stop to explain.

There were only a few guests at the bar being attended to by one of the new bartenders. Jason was sitting at the piano. He wasn't playing but leaning forward studying a pile of papers spread out on the music stand. She walked up behind him.

Seeing the papers were music, she said in a teasing manner, "Is this is why you wanted me to come down here right away, to play this for you?"

He gave her a quick look with a smile before refocusing on the sheets of music. "This is a new piece I have never heard or played."

"Where did you get it?"

Jason did a quick survey of the room, making sure no one was in hearing distance. "It's a piano concerto Uncle Andy wrote. It's never been performed."

"Why did he give it to you?"

Jason stared at the score. "He said he had never found anyone he could trust to play it the way he intended."

"Wow," Noel said. "That's something. You should be honored."

"I am."

Noel laid her arm across his shoulder. "Why did you call me to come down here?"

Jason looked up at her. "This is a special moment. I wanted to share it with you."

Noel leaned forward. "Thank you." She kissed him on the cheek. Straightening up, she continued. "So, are you going to play it?"

Jason let out a nervous chuckle. "I'm going to try."

"Let me ask you something," Noel said. "How do you approach learning a piece like this?"

"It depends on the degree of difficulty," Jason said, pausing. "With this one, I'll probably play it the whole way through, identifying areas that need more work than others."

"How difficult is this?" Noel asked.

Jason flipped through a couple pages. "Technically, there are areas that are complex. However, interpretation is going to be the key."

"And Uncle Andy thought you are the person who can do that?"

"That's what he said."

Noel pointed to the pages on the music stand. "Then go ahead and turn this into a beautiful piece of music." She stopped but quickly added. "By the way, what's it called? What's its name?"

Jason organized the pages from left to right. "It's untitled."

"Oh."

Jason said nothing else as he focused on the first page.

. . . . .

Hands poised above the keys, Jason took a couple of deep breaths and began to play. Noel moved to the bar where she ordered an iced tea. She turned her stool to watch and listen. She knew little about classical music, but she quickly knew that what she was hearing was a masterpiece being born. She also knew it was a master pianist giving birth to this composition.

When Bobby came on duty a short time later, he was quick to sense the atmosphere. Noel told him Jason was working on a new piece, presumably for his recital. As was his custom when he first arrived, Bobby wiped down the bar from one end to the other.

As he got back to Noel, he said, "Sounds wonderful to me."

"Me, too."

The music continued.

. . . . .

Some thirty minutes later, Jason went through the last series of progression up and down the keyboard. It was fast, it was powerful, yet very melodical. The final chord run, and it was finished. Jason sat with his head bent down, his hands on his knees. He took a couple deep breaths. There was a long moment of silence, then he heard noise. The noise gradually increased in volume. He looked to his right. The tables in the dining room remained empty for the most part, however, a crowd had gathered at the bar and numerous people stood in the perimeter of the room. Everyone was on their feet applauding.

Jason rose to his feet and thanked the crowd. The applause continued for another half minute before slowly fading away.

Jason looked toward the bar. Noel and Bobby were also applauding. He made eye contact with Noel who smiled and gave him two thumbs up. Jason took another bow before heading to the end of the bar where Bobby had a tall glass of water waiting for him.

. . . . .

Noel watched as Jason received the applause and accolades he justly deserved. When the applause subsided, he came over to the bar where he downed a glass of water. He said his hellos before returning to the piano where he played a medley of standards and modern-day songs he had been working on, followed by several other classical pieces for the recital. The crowd was appreciative. The tip bucket was half-full. As time passed and the crowd thinned out, Noel made her way to the piano. Seeing her coming, he rose to his feet and held out his arms. They hugged for a long moment.

Noel was unable to hold back the tears. "I don't know what to say."

"I'll take that as a compliment," Jason said. "Thank you."

"No, thank you. Thank you for calling and asking me to come down here," Noel said. She wiped her hand across her eyes. "I witnessed something magical tonight."

Jason's eyebrows rose. "I'm not sure I would go that far."

"You weren't standing in the back watching you, watching the crowd and listening. You've wowed the crowd before, but tonight they were…." She paused to come up with the right word. "They were hypnotized. So was I."

Jason took a long swallow of water Noel had brought him. "I think playing the piece the whole way through the first time worked well," he said.

"What do you think of it?" Noel asked.

"Overall, it's a powerful yet beautiful piece of music. It's full of life and full of passion." Jason paused for another swallow of water. "There is a section in the middle of the second movement I don't understand, but it'll come to me."

"I thought you played it well," Noel complimented.

Jason shrugged. "Some sections, yes. Others need a lot of work. But that's not unusual when learning a new piece."

"What do you think Uncle Andy is trying to do with this piece?" Noel asked.

"I think he's telling a story of his time here in Baddeck," Jason said. "Strolling through town, walking along the waterfront, being on the boat with Uncle Henry. The common theme through it all is the wind in his face, which fluctuates throughout the piece. Luckily, and because I played it all the way through the first time, I was able to recognize the story quickly, which will help as I work on the interpretation. Although, again, there's that one section that is somewhat baffling."

"I'm sure you will figure it out," Noel said.

"Hopefully."

"Anyway, I'll leave you alone so you can practice," Noel said, starting to step away.

Jason reached up and grabbed her arm. "How about I meet you upstairs in say, forty minutes?"

Noel smiled. "That'll give me time to do a couple things first."

"Something to do? I thought you were off today?" Jason said innocently.

Noel leaned into him and spoke softly. "I need to get some shampoos and little soaps."

. . . . .

Noel lay on her back, her forearm across her head, eyes closed. Her heart was pounding in her chest. A smile crossed her face. She could hear the shower running in the bathroom. She turned her head slightly to the side to look at the clock on the bedside table. Five minutes after six. Plenty of time for a shower, but she'd be cutting it close for work.

She rose to her feet, making her way quickly to the bathroom before Jason turned off the water. So as not to startle him, she tapped on the door lightly.

"May I join you?"

She heard him laugh. "Come on in."

She pushed open the door and walked in. Hot steam greeted her. The clear glass shower enclosure was covered in mist as well. He slid the door open and held out his hand. She dropped the towel she had wrapped around herself and stepped in.

"Morning, Sunshine," Jason said, stepping back so she could get under the shower head. She faced him and leaned her head back. The water felt good. Jason moved closer and wrapped his arms around her waist. He pulled her into him. She let out a soft moan. He kissed her exposed neck, his tongue tickling her in areas where she never knew she was ticklish. His kisses moved downward. When they reached her breast, she let out a soft moan. At the same time, a bolt of electricity shot through her body. She grabbed his head and pulled him up to her. She kissed him passionately.

Yes, she'd be cutting it close for work.

CHAPTER 27

Before Jason realized it, spring had eased into summer. The weather went from warm and pleasant to downright hot. If it wasn't for an afternoon breeze coming off the mountains, it would have been even worse. The occasional short-lived afternoon showers were of little help. If anything, the humidity that followed was even higher.

With Baddeck being in the Cabot Trail, the town served as a hub for those anxious to explore the area. Tourists arrived, creating a very busy atmosphere for the town and the Baddeck Cottage. Luckily, the summer help, locals plus those from abroad, arrived on time and with enthusiasm. There was plenty of work to go around and there was ample overtime for those who wanted it. At the cottage, there were problems, as would be expected, but thanks to Gabbey and her staff, each was addressed expediently and efficiently.

The tourists didn't complain, taking it all in stride, getting up early to have breakfast and getting to their buses on time for their daily excursions. With Alex busy taking care of maintenance issues, Noel took over most of the local touring activities. Bobby even helped out where he could during the day, driving the van to free up Noel to do the hiking expeditions.

If there was room, Jason would go with Noel on the hiking expeditions. He never tired of the excursions. There was always something new to experience. Even though physical at times, Jason found hiking to be emotionally relaxing. He even enjoyed the occasional trip up to the fire tower, which was now fully staffed and active. The serenity and beauty of the mountains did wonders to help reduce his anxiety about the upcoming recital.

Another benefit, he got to spend time with Noel.

During this time, Jason continued to work diligently on his recital prep. Gabbey gave him the okay to play anytime he wanted as long as he paid some attention to the guests. He had no problem with this, as for the most part the guests were appreciative of the entertainment. If asked, he answered honestly that he was in school for music and was here preparing for his graduate recital.

As guests came and went, Jason's reputation grew, and there were more and more people choosing to eat dinner at the cottage to hear the young pianist. If they didn't eat dinner there, they often stopped by the bar for a night cap and to hear him play. Jason was quickly making a name for himself.

Gabbey stopped by one afternoon while Jason was practicing. She stood off to the side listening, continuing to be amazed at his talent as well as his versatility. She didn't know much about classical music; she did know that being able to mix classics with standards and modern-day hits was an art in itself. He did it with such finesse.

When he noticed her, he stopped and looked her way. "Everything okay?"

"Just stopped by to see how you were doing," Gabbey said. "Haven't talked to you recently."

"This is the first afternoon in a while I haven't been hiking with Noel," he said.

Gabbey tipped her head to the side. She gave him a soft smile, swallowing any comments about their relationship, which she had watched blossom over the past weeks.

"I'm sure she appreciates the help."

"I enjoy spending time with her and helping where I can," Jason said.

Stepping in closer, Gabbey said, "I wanted to talk to you about your playing, specifically the work you're doing in the evening."

"Is there a problem?" Jason said with concern.

"Absolutely not," Gabbey said quickly. "On the contrary, you're having a positive impact on our business."

Jason spun around on the piano bench so he was facing her. "I appreciate the opportunity to practice."

Gabbey cleared her throat. "I'm thinking I need to pay you for your services."

Jason rose to his feet and twisted to work out a kink in his back. "I play for free. I'm not willing to change that."

"But..."

Jason stepped toward and put his arms on Gabbey's shoulders. His stern expression turned into one of pleasure.

"Listen, Gabbey, I should be paying you for use of the piano and allowing me to practice in front of your guests. I've had some great experiences, met some great people... you included...and my playing has drastically improved. I've learned how to find myself in the music."

Gabbey smiled. "Okay. Let's leave it this way: if ever you feel you want compensation, let me know."

Jason gave her a big grin. "I'd like to continue with the tip bucket."

Gabbey put her hand across her mouth to subdue a laugh. "I know you give that money to the staff every night." She paused. "I also know about your relationship with Noel. I just hope…."

Before she could say anything, Jason spoke softly. "No need to say anymore. For the record, what Noel and I have is much more than a summer romance." He paused briefly. "We care deeply about each other."

Gabbey was glad she didn't have to vocalize what she had been thinking about just now, which was not wanting to see Noel hurt again. She had grown fond of Jason as well and didn't want to do or say anything that would interfere in their relationship.

Gabbey and Noel's mother were in frequent contact. Like Gabbey, Noel's mother had similar concerns about the young girl getting hurt. Jason meeting her and Gabbey's overwhelming positive comments went a long way to alleviate her concerns. She'd told Gabbey that her initial impression of Jason had been very positive, a comment Gabbey had never heard the woman make before. Gabbey planned to talk to Noel's mother again later and would pass along her own thoughts that were reinforced the last couple minutes.

Aloud, Gabbey said, "I've taken enough of your practice time. Thank you for entertaining our guests. Again, if you change your mind about compensation…." Jason lifted his hand to stop her. She gave him a nod of understanding. "If you need anything, I'm here for you."

"There is one thing," Jason said, causing her to pause as she started to walk away. "How late or early can I play?"

"If you're concerned about bothering guests late at night or early in the morning, don't be," Gabbey said. "As long as you don't use amplifiers, the banquet rooms and lounge area are pretty soundproof. She paused. "You thinking of practicing at night?"

"I need to focus on the pieces for the recital. That involves a lot of concentration as well as a lot of starting and stopping."

"I have no problem with you working at night," Gabbey said.

"I used to practice a lot at night at school," Jason explained. "A lot fewer distractions."

Gabbey let out a chuckle. "I'll let the night security staff know you may be wondering around at all hours."

"I appreciate that."

"I'm sure they'll appreciate a little entertainment as well," Gabbey said. She nodded and walked away.

. . . . .

With the okay to practice anytime of the day, Jason converted to the schedule he followed his first two years at Barrett Conservatory, which included a lot of early morning/late night sessions. Through it all, however, he ensured he got his rest, something stressed by his instructors. "You must be at the top of your game on stage, and you cannot be at the top of your game if you are not well rested."

The ability to rest and rejuvenate his body in short spurts was something he learned from his father, who spent long hours in front of computer screens constantly watching the financial markets of the world.

With this schedule adjustment, the month of June passed quickly. While not fixed in stone, his daily routine was only interrupted on days he went hiking with Noel, which he tried to do at least once a week. He kept reminding himself why he came to Baddeck and what he had gained since being here. He definitely didn't want to lose that.

Jason's and Noel's time together except for hikes in the mountains became limited. Besides doing the hiking tours, Noel was kept busy helping Gabbey doing whatever it took to keep things at the cottage running smoothly. There was also an occasional call from Uncle Henry who needed an extra hand. She and Cindy also had their summer schoolwork, which took time as well. Jason had his own papers to work on, which he often did in the early morning hours out on the patio when taking a break from practicing.

There were times, however, when Jason's sleep was interrupted by a soft tapping on his door. He'd open it to find Noel standing there with a couple bottles of shampoo and little bars of soap. Her visits, not nearly as frequent as each would have liked, would disrupt his schedule, but he never complained.

CHAPTER 28

As the beginning of July neared, Jason had to remind himself he was in Canada, and they didn't celebrate the 4th of July, although a large percentage of tourists were from the US. He overheard several people asking Gabbey what the Baddeck Cottage did for the 4th. Gabbey said they didn't do anything special, including no fireworks because of the risk of forest fires. He had to chuckle to himself as this was in dire contrast to what would be going on in New York City during this time.

It was Jason who came up with the idea of celebrating an international day versus a specific Independence Day. "The 4th of July is a big picnic day. Let's have a picnic," he said one afternoon when Cookie and Noel were in the lounge listening to him practice. "Hamburgers and hot dogs plus other international fair." Cookie especially liked the idea of being able to diversify from the normal menu.

Gabbey, who had been standing off to the side listening to this conversation, stepped forward. "I'll make a couple calls to our suppliers in Halifax to see what they can come up with." Looking directly at Cookie, she added, "Let's hold off publicizing the menu until we know what's available."

"Let's make it easy," Cookie said. "No menu. We'll just cook what we can get and put it out as a buffet."

"Make it real casual. It'll look like a real picnic," Jason suggested.

One of the line cooks, a young college girl named Julia, who had come out to listen as well, spoke up. She was short, petite, with a perky voice and personality.

"America's 4th of July picnics are hamburgers and hot dogs, right?" she asked. When no one disagreed, she continued. "Let's fix hamburgers and hot dogs but set out a variety of different sauces and condiments that would be common to international foods. We can also make different kinds of salads specific to specific areas. And we can make a variety of pastries for dessert."

"Great idea," Gabbey said. She glanced at Cookie, giving him a *what-do-you-think* look.

Cookie draped his arm over the girl's shoulder. "I've got the best staff, even though they can be a real pain at times."

He started to give her a fatherly hug but quickly turned it into a gentle push toward the kitchen.

Looking over her shoulder, Julie said with a laugh, "See how he treats us, Gabbey?"

. . . . .

The picnic was scheduled to begin around four in the afternoon, with off-site activities on that particular day planned for the morning. The thunderstorms that have been predicted decided to hold off for the celebration. There was a gentle breeze throughout the day, helping make the heat tolerable. The menu was a hit, with hamburgers and hot dogs cooked on an outside grill just like an American picnic. There were salads, sauces, and condiments, each with a different international flair, each with a place card depicting what it was and the country it represented. There was plenty of iced tea and lemonade. The bar was open, and Bobby created a variety of drink specials. While the main food was a hit, the table receiving the most praise was the array of desserts from different countries Julie had prepared. The most popular was a dessert from Portugal called pasties de nata, a puff pastry filled with a delicious vanilla custard. Jason was happy to provide the entertainment when the piano was wheeled out onto the patio. Guests could listen to Jason play while watching the kaleidoscope of colors in the sky as the sun slowly descended. It was a perfect evening.

Cindy took photographs on her phone throughout the day. A couple of the photographs in particular turned out to be majestic and wonderful. They would later be blown up, framed, and given to Gabbey as a Christmas present by the staff.

It was after midnight before the picnic/party finally broke up. The staff were quick to clean up, get everything in order, including moving the piano back inside. Jason went to his room after saying goodbye to the guests, thanking the staff for a great time, and handing the over-flowing tip bucket to Bobby. Jason fell across the bed completely dressed. He was sleeping soundly when he heard a tapping. He rose to his feet and shuffled to the door. Noel looked as tired as he felt. Her hair was a mess. Her clothes were wrinkled and stained. Despite it all, she still looked beautiful.

He grabbed her arm and pulled her through the door, closing it behind them. He then pressed her up against the wall and greeted her with a passionate kiss.

"You're a mess," he whispered in her ear. "You smell..." He paused as he sniffed her neck.

Noel let out a tired giggle. "I smell like hamburgers and hot dogs."

"Well, we'll just have to do something about that," he said, leading her toward the bathroom.

. . . . .

A steady breeze blew through the open window, causing the curtains to sway side to side as they let the sunlight in sporadically. Noel instinctively put her arm across her eyes to block the light. She slowly awoke, becoming more cognizant of her surroundings. She rolled to her side and laid her arm across Jason's chest.

Jason's eyes opened. "Morning, Glory," he said with a sleepy grin.

"Good morning," she repeated.

They kissed, easily at first, and then more passionately. They both let out a soft moan. He reached over and pulled her on top of him.

"Oh, my," she said as he slid into her.

Later, they sat together on the edge of the bed, Noel with a towel wrapped around her chest, Jason with a towel around his waist.

"You don't have much time left, do you?" Noel said softly, leaning her head on Jason's shoulder.

Jason thought for a moment. "Beginning of September... about eight weeks." He pulled his hand through her hair.

"Remember, summer will be ending, but that'll be the beginning of our future."

"How will *our future* look?" Noel pressed.

Jason understood it was the *unknown* Noel struggled with, as he had similar concerns. "Neither of us know what the future is going to bring. What I do know is that we want our journeys to be as close to one another as possible. There are going to be obstacles to navigate around as we each embark on our careers. It will be difficult to be apart, but we can look forward to the time we will be back together. And when we are together, it will be wonderful."

Jason watched Noel hold back the tears. He had never seen her look so sad.

"We still have eight weeks," he said softly.

"Are you always this positive?" she asked, wiping her forearm across her eyes.

"If you start off negatively, you will never succeed. With a positive attitude, you have a chance. It's similar to how I attack a new piece of music."

Jason pulled her back on the bed. He rolled on top of her, careful to keep his weight off. Looking deep into her eyes, he said, "Here's what's going to happen. Each time we see each other, I'm going to give you a kiss and tell you that I am madly in love with you." He removed her towel. "When we're alone…" He began spreading kisses down her body. When he finished, he scooted up so he could again kiss her on the lips.

Noel wrapped her arms around his neck and pulled him to her. "My turn."

. . . . .

The talk among the guests over the next couple of days was how wonderful the International Day picnic was. The praise the cottage received re-energized the staff to face the rest of the summer.

Alex came out to the patio two afternoons later while Jason was taking a break from practicing.

Pounding him gently on the back, Alex said, "You were a hit, my friend. I don't know what your future holds as far as your music, but I do have good ears, and I listen well. You should be very proud." He gave Jason another back pat.

Jason looked at Alex, whom he had become fond of both as a friend and a mentor. The man always spoke softly and with a smile, and his words always heartfelt and meaningful. His telling Jason he should be proud struck a nerve. The young pianist could not recall anyone ever telling him that before.

All Jason could verbalize was a thank you. Alex nodded and walked away. Jason finished his iced tea and headed back to the lounge. As the piano came into view, he smiled as he thought of a popular saying by one of his instructors. "Remember, playing an instrument is a dance that requires two."

Gently tapping the top of the piano, Jason mouthed softly, "Are you ready to dance?"

CHAPTER 29

Jason and Noel continued to be busy the next couple of weeks. Both were busy during the day. At night, Jason focused on practicing while Noel focused on her schoolwork. She was pleased that she and Cindy were both on schedule to complete their program by the end of the summer. Everyone knew though, this was a busy time for the Baddeck Cottage and a pressure time for Jason's recital prep. Noel and Jason took all this in stride, always ending their time together with a kiss followed by a few words of love and affection.

Jason's two papers were completed and turned in electronically. He was happy with his recital prep. He was especially pleased with how Uncle Andy's piano concerto was progressing; except he continued to have difficulty interpreting the middle section of the second movement. He was convinced there was a missing part of the story. Unfortunately, Uncle Andy wasn't available to consultation as he was touring throughout Australia.

Jason played the piece through one evening, finishing just as Bobby was closing out for the night. Jason pulled the cover of the keyboard and walked up to the bar.

Sliding a glass of water forward, Bobby said, "Sounds good. The new piece is coming along, too, don't you think?"

Jason drank half the water. "More or less. I'm having trouble with the second movement. It almost seems out of place, or there's something missing."

Bobby topped off Jason's water glass. "If it's the area I'm thinking of, it's like it comes on suddenly and disappears suddenly."

"Exactly," Jason agreed.

"Your whole persona changes during that section," Bobby said.

"That obvious, eh?"

The bartender shrugged. "I like to people watch." He finished wiping down the bar. "We'll get out of here in a second so you can get back to work figuring it out."

Jason looked around and saw Freddie and Allen sitting at a table patiently. "Hey guys, how you doing?" he said, walking over to the pair. He gave them each a high five. "And… what are you doing here this time of the night?"

"Uncle Bobby's taking us pirate hunting," Allen said excitedly. "They only come out at midnight when the moon is full."

"Pirates?" Jason asked.

"You never heard of the Midnight Pirates of Baddeck?" Freddie asked.

Jason gave Bobby a puzzled look. "Can't say that I have."

"The locals don't talk about the pirates much, for fear of chasing the tourists away," Bobby explained.

"I see," Jason said, catching the twinkle in the bartender/pirate hunter's eye.

"Wanna come with us?" Allen said hopefully.

"Yes, the more pirate hunters, the better the chance of catching 'em," Freddie added.

It took Jason only a moment to decide to hunt pirates versus practice the piano. Walking up behind the two boys, he gave them a gentle shove. “Okay, guys, let’s go catch some pirates!”

. . . . .

The moon was full, the sky overcast. The light filtering through the clouds painted the town with an assortment of grays. Mixed in with the few streetlights were shadows appearing to wave in the breeze. According to the two boys, it was a perfect night to hunt pirates.

Ordering a single file, Bobby led the way into town. The two boys were in the middle. Jason brought up the rear. They had no protection other than the running shoes they wore. They made their way up and down the streets, ducking in and out of alleyways, staying alert and keeping as quiet as possible. Whenever Bobby commented he might have heard something suspicious, the boys always agreed they’d heard it too.

They had been walking for a while when Bobby stopped. He gathered the boys around him. Leaning into them, he whispered, “It’s getting close to midnight, so we need to be especially alert.”

Suddenly, there was total silence. A hooting owl stopped. The wind died out. The foursome stood still, the boys showing increased nervousness. Bobby looked at Jason and gave him a slight head nod. There was enough light Jason could read Bobby’s lips. “Be patient,” he mouthed silently.

Just as suddenly, the wind returned, slowly at first, and

then with intermittent gusts. The light from the moon disappeared as the clouds thickened. Then they heard it, a soft whistling howl at first, and then it increased in pitch and intensity. The pirates had arrived!

"They're going that way," Bobby shouted, this time unconcerned about the volume of his voice. He took off running back the way they had just come. The three pirate hunters behind him followed. Bobby looked over his shoulder as he ran, making sure he didn't get too far ahead of the boys. "Watch your steps," he directed. "The pirates may have laid down some booby traps."

The whistling noise increased in intensity as they approached one of the larger houses on the block. Stopping in front, Bobby pointed in that direction. "They're on the porch!" Bobby said with excitement.

"What do we do?" the boys said simultaneously. "We can't go in someone's yard."

Bobby pretended to contemplate the question for a moment. "We'll wait. They have to come off the porch sooner or later. Then we'll grab 'em!" He waved his arms in both directions. "Spread out boys."

The pirates suddenly stopped howling. The clouds uncovered the moon letting light come down into the area. The wind again died out. What had seemed like a battle about to break out was now an eerie silence.

"What happened?" one of the boys said.

"They must have escaped," Bobby said, scanning the area in front of the house.

"Escaped! How?"

"Probably over the roof into the backyard. From there, they could have gone anywhere."

"Can we go after them?"

"We don't know which way they went," Bobby said.

Both boys let out deep sighs of disappointment.

"I'm sorry," Bobby said. "We'll get them next time, eh?"

Not needing a lot of encouragement, both boys headed back uphill toward the cottage. Bobby let them get half a block ahead.

Looking at Jason, he said, "So, what did you think?'

"It was fun watching the boys' reactions. Thanks for letting me tag along," Jason said.

"Anytime," Bobby said.

"How'd you come up with this anyway?" Jason asked.

"It's a story Uncle Andy has been telling around here for years," Bobby said. "He complains all the time about pirates running around his house."

Jason stopped and looked back over his shoulder. "You mean...."

"Yeah. Uncle Andy's. Whose house do you think we were at?"

"I didn't recognize the place at night."

"A lot of these older homes look different in the dark."

Still walking behind the boys, Jason asked, "What were we hearing?"

"When the wind comes directly off the lake, it hits the front of Uncle Andy's house and rattles the shutters. Uncle Andy said it's always been musical, but as the wood has aged, the sound has changed. Still musical, but now a little spooky, too. We were lucky tonight the wind hit when it did."

"Instead of ghosts, he came up with a pirate story?" Jason said.

"Exactly."

Jason took a couple more steps before stopping suddenly. He turned and again looked down the street. He could barely make out the top of the house as it was taller than others in the area. "Musical and spooky," he said aloud. He looked at Bobby. "That's it," he said, excitement filling his voice. "That's the answer."

CHAPTER 30

A week later, Jason walked into the lounge at closing time. He carried his iPad and a folder of papers in one hand and a bottle of water in the other. He looked rested and ready for a long night of practice. He stopped by the bar and grabbed the glass of ice Bobby had set up for him. Greetings were exchanged and Jason moved to the piano. A short time later, music filled the empty room.

Bobby was just leaving for the night when he saw Uncle Andy sit down at the bar. The maestro put his finger up to his lips, asking for silence. Bobby nodded and headed into the kitchen. Uncle Andy slid up onto a bar stool.

Jason continued to play, oblivious to his audience. Fifteen minutes later, Jason paused for a drink of water. He opened the folder and set the pages on the music stand. With minimal hesitation, he began playing the first notes of Andrew Summer's Piano Concerto #1 in G minor. Jason played it straight through, making mental notes of the areas he wanted to work on later. When he came to the area in the second movement where he had been having difficulty, he adjusted his posture slightly and told himself to go for it. He had pirates to catch.

His heart rate increased. His excitement built as he attacked the section with new found intensity. At the same time, he made sure he kept his overall tone in check. He made it through the section, thrilled with his play technically, as well as his interpretation. The rest of the piece flowed relatively smoothly from there. He finished with a flourish, representing the sun just cropping over the top of the eastern mountain range. Andrew Summer's nighttime stroll through the town of Baddeck, including a brief confrontation with pirates, was complete.

Jason's hands hovered over the keys a moment before dropping to his lap. His head bowed; his eyes closed. The room was silent.

But only for a moment. Jason's head snapped up at the sound of a single person's applause. He spun on the bench and looked toward the bar. Uncle Andy was standing next to a stool, a wide smile on his face, clapping his hands in a slow fashion. Jason rose to his feet, unsure what to say or do.

"I would yell bravo, but that might disturb the guests," Uncle Andy said. He moved toward the piano. "I have listened to hundreds of students in my time, but your ability is amazing…utterly amazing."

"Thank you," Jason said, wiping perspiration from his forehead. Still unsure what to say, he continued with, "How'd your tour go?"

"Excellent," Uncle Andy replied. "Australia is huge. The country is beautiful, and the people knowledgeable and appreciative."

"That's wonderful."

"Thank you." Uncle Andy laid his hand atop the piano. "But I didn't come here to talk about Australia. I came to listen to you." He paused briefly. "You really are doing justice to the concerto."

The overwhelming question in Jason's mind quickly surfaced. "Am I interrupting it as you envisioned?"

The composer smiled. "It was wonderful."

Jason's eyebrows rose. "Wow."

Uncle Andy continued. "I did wonder how you would handle the middle section of the second movement."

Jason smiled. "I went on a pirate hunt with Bobby and the two boys."

Uncle Andy chuckled. "Did you enjoy yourself?"

"We didn't catch any pirates, but the wind was musical... and spooky."

They talked a few minutes about the concerto and Jason's playing thereof, and then Uncle Andy headed home.

"Watch out for the pirates," Jason warned in jest.

"They know better than to mess with me," the maestro said without looking back.

CHAPTER 31

Noel looked at the calendar lying on her office desk. Her office was small, but thanks to Alex's wife's help with decorating, it was homey and comfortable. The office was adjacent to Gabbey's, giving Noel easy access to her boss and mentor. There was a large window with a view of the mountains during the daytime. Tonight, with the window open to let in the breeze, it was dark outside.

Noel continued staring at the calendar. It was forty days before Jason was to leave. She was already missing him. She knew it was going to be worse with him gone. She told herself not to despair. First Nation people were strong.

She thought about how her mother handled the death of her father. Her mother mourned, but at the same time, she remained strong for her children. Noel wished her mother was here to help her now. She could use some of that strength.

. . . . .

Jason lay on his back, staring at the ceiling, his arms folded behind his head. His body was tired. His mind, however, was wide awake. He took a deep breath as his thoughts turned to the past few hours. Uncle Andy had heard his concerto from start to finish and was delighted with Jason's interpretation and play. That he had made no negative comment or criticism and only made a few suggestions in areas Jason asked about, was a compliment in itself. It was certainly a weight off Jason's shoulders. The question now: what was he going to do with the piece? Jason wanted to use it for his recital and felt Barrett's concert hall would be a great venue to premiere such a wonderful piece of music. But despite Uncle Andy being pleased with the concerto thus far, both knew it was not yet performance-ready. Jason had plenty of other material prepared for the recital. They had decided to wait and see how things progressed. In the meantime, Jason would continue working on the piece along with other selections. Uncle Andy, however, did recommend that Jason take a few days off again.

Jason rolled toward the window, feeling the breeze on his face. He'd missed waking up with Noel the past few nights. Their schedules were just too hectic. He missed her emotionally. He missed her physically. As he rolled onto his back, he thought about the additional days off. He didn't want to do anything to interfere with Noel's work. His thoughts turned to something he had been thinking of lately but had pushed aside, telling himself it was too soon for such an idea. He told himself he had to think that through very carefully. Don't be impulsive, he warned.

He sat up and broke into a wide smile. Their relationship started with an impulsive decision. Why not continue the trend?

CHAPTER 32

The next morning, Jason hurried down the hill towards the harbor. There was a slight breeze falling off the mountain, causing the lake's surface to show gentle ripples in response. A few ducks could be seen along the water's edge searching for their breakfast. With a clear sky, it was a beautiful summer Canadian morning.

When Jason came to the waterfront, he saw there were already cars in the parking lot and activity along the waterfront. People were out sightseeing or heading to The Box On The Dock for breakfast. As he rounded the corner, he saw *My First Lady III* in the distance.

Uncle Henry was on the dock unloading a handcart of bar supplies. The boat captain looked up as Jason approached. Recognizing the young man, he broke into a smile. "Morning, Jason. What are you doing out and about so early?"

"Actually, I came to see you," Jason said, shaking the man's hand.

Uncle Henry straightened up and worked a kink out of his back. "What can I do for you?"

"I was hoping we could talk. I have a couple questions," Jason said hesitantly.

"Are these quick questions?"

"The questions are quick. I'm not sure about the answers," Jason admitted with a shrug.

"I'm expecting a couple busses of tourists in a few minutes. So, I have to get this stuff on board and put away." Captain Henry tipped his head to the side. "Wanna come along? We can talk then."

Jason smiled. "Sounds like a fine way to spend the morning."

Captain Henry pointed at the boxes. "Help me with this stuff, eh?"

. . . . .

When they got back to the dock later that morning, Jason went up to the cottage to find Noel and tell her he was taking a few days to tour around the region himself. He knew she was swamped with tours and other tasks, so their time together would be limited anyway.

Jason couldn't find Noel, but Gabbey was in her office. She told him Noel was out on a hiking tour and wouldn't be back till later in the afternoon. She said it was a late add on. Jason explained his plan for his days off. Gabbey thought it was a wonderful idea and offered Jason her Jeep.

Several hours later as the last light left the sky, Jason pulled onto the property of his first destination and followed signs to guest parking. He took a moment to stretch as he locked the car. Rounding the corner of the building, he saw the casino's entrance. A security guard was checking ID's. Jason had his driver's license and passport out. The guard gave them a quick look before waving him through. Inside, the building was full of lights and noise. Jason paused to allow his senses to adjust to the sensory overload. He had only been to a casino a couple times in his life and never gambled away more than a few dollars with each visit.

But Jason wasn't here to gamble. He was here to meet Noel's older brother.

As he was walking through the lobby, he saw a tall, muscular First Nation man walking toward him. He was dressed in a tailored blue suit. He wore a white shirt with a stylish red necktie. His feet were covered in a pair of polished boots. His long black hair was braided and hung to his waist. He was well built and quite handsome.

The man came right up to him and held out his hand. "Mr. Kinde?"

Jason took the hand. "Yes, that's me."

"John Liam Summers. I go by Lee. It's a pleasure to meet you. Noel has told me a lot about you."

"It's a pleasure to meet you as well," Jason returned. "Noel has also told me about you."

Lee smiled. "Believe only the good parts." He continued after a brief pause. "You called and said you wanted to meet and that you have some questions."

"That's correct," Jason said. "Thanks for taking my call earlier, by the way."

"No problem, but to be honest, Uncle Henry gave me a heads up."

"You know Uncle Henry?"

Lee let out a soft chuckle. "Everybody knows Uncle Henry." He turned slightly and pointed across the floor toward the left. "Follow me, and we'll go somewhere we can talk in private."

Jason nodded and did as he was told.

. . . . .

When finished visiting with Noel's brother, Jason headed to the motel Lee had recommended. It wasn't anything fancy, but it was clean, and rooms were available. After checking in, Jason walked to a diner across the street where he ate a very tasty lobster roll along with a local craft beer. As he stared at one of the televisions without sound, his mind kept going back to the earlier conversations with Uncle Henry and Noel's brother. They were good conversations, giving him confidence in what he was doing. Although, he still had one more person to see before returning to the cottage. Naturally, there was some apprehension, yet he felt in his heart he was doing the right thing.

Returning to his room, he took a shower and laid across the bed where he fell asleep a short time later. When he woke up with the sun the next morning, he dressed in his running clothes and headed out the door. An hour later he was in the diner across the street having breakfast. A short time after that, he was back on the road driving south toward his next destination.

CHAPTER 33

Noel lay with her back toward the open window, the warm breeze messaging her sore muscles. It had been a vigorous yet satisfying day and she was tired. Still, she planned to get up early the next morning and head to the pool.

She was about to roll over when her cell phone buzzed. She picked up the phone and saw a text from Jason. She tapped the screen. She read it quickly. A smile formed as fast. *Just got back. Need some hugs and kisses. Luv, JK.*

Noel dressed quickly in a tee shirt and shorts and headed out the door. She made her way via a storage closet where she picked up a handful of toiletries.

. . . . .

Noel left Jason's room early the next morning with a smile on her face. After a steamy shower when she first arrived, they made love once before falling asleep in each other's arms. The alarm on Noel's phone was the next thing either one heard.

As the door closed, Jason flopped back on the bed. After a moment, he decided to join her in the pool. Noel was already there when he arrived. He waited until she was at the far end before jumping in so as not to startle her. She still heard him and stopped. She waved and swam toward him.

Taking a quick look around to make sure they were alone, she grabbed the arms he held out for her.

Wrapping her legs around his waist, she said, "Good morning. You sleep okay?"

"Yes," he said, pressing into her firmly.

Noel leaned back and said, "Jason, I just left you."

"And now you're hugging me wearing a sexy, tight-fitting bathing suit," Jason countered, trying to pull her back to him.

"You've seen me in this before. It's designed for swimming."

He leaned in, gave her a quick kiss, and said, "It's also designed for teasing your boyfriend."

She gave him a wide smile. "That sounds nice. Thank you."

"I love you," Jason said.

"I love you, too."

Splashes at the far end of the pool followed by the sound of children squealing broke the mood. That was okay though, they had had their moment.

. . . . .

Donald Kinde scanned the center computer screen, looked at the monitor on the right and then the one on the left. The information he was getting from three different programs didn't add up. Something was going on in China's stock exchanges, and he hadn't figured it out yet. The fact that there were conflicts showing up between three different systems gave him even more concern.

He again scanned the computer screens. What was he missing? Several minutes passed, then he saw it. Someone was purposely trying to manipulate the markets. It was subtle, but it was there. He pulled the keyboard toward him and started typing. Three minutes later he moved his hands away from the keyboard and carefully checked what he had typed. He took a deep breath and hit the send button.

He took another deep breath. He knew that within minutes the brokers and financial advisors that work for his firm would be pulling out billions of dollars from the three main China markets. "Manipulate away," he uttered, "but not with our money."

He picked up the cup of coffee he had started six hours earlier. It was cold, as was the norm. He took a long swallow. As he sat the cup down, his cell phone buzzed. Without looking to see who it was, he hit the speaker button. "You can thank me in about a half an hour when the China markets start to decline," he said. "Don't worry, though, they'll recover in a couple of days."

"Well, I hope you got our money out before this happens," Jason said.

Donald quickly glanced at the display on the phone. Seeing it was his son verses who he was thinking, he broke into a smile. "I took your sister's money out, but left yours alone," he quipped.

"Dad!"

"Don't worry, Jason, I don't have any of our money in China right now."

"Anyway, how are you, Dad?" Jason said, making a

mental note to check the financial news later to see what his father was talking about.

"We're all good. You?"

"Baddeck is amazing," Jason said.

"How is the hotel? Are you being treated well?"

"Wonderful and very well."

"How 'bout your playing?"

"From what everyone has said, that has improved. I, myself, feel very satisfied. I'm also very appreciative of the opportunity to be here," Jason said.

"Your mother and I are happy it's working out," Donald said. Thinking it was unusual hearing from Jason in the middle of the day, his father quickly added, "Is everything okay?"

"Everything's fine." Jason paused before continuing. "What are you and Mom doing next weekend?"

Jason's father frowned. His son knew what was happening the next weekend as it had been the same for multiple years. "We're going to Martha's Vineyard like we always do. Your mother and sister are in Paris but will be home tomorrow night."

Jason again paused. "I need you to change your plans. Come up to Baddeck to see the place and meet the people."

David Kinde immediately recognized there was more to the invitation than Baddeck being a wonderful place to visit. He knew his son well and was pretty sure he already knew the reason. When the call ended a short time later, he opened the photo file on his phone and scrolled down to the pictures Jason had recently sent. Stopping at one photo of his son standing next to a beautiful native-looking girl, he said aloud, "I bet it is an amazing place."

He broke into a smile as he finished his cold coffee and turned his attention back to the computer screens. The China markets were already reacting.

CHAPTER 34

The following Sunday morning awoke with a kaleidoscope of colors flowing over the top of the eastern mountains. The sky was clear. The sun reflected off the Bras d'Or Lake's glass-like surface. It was going to be a beautiful, yet hot and muggy mid-August day.

There was activity on the dock around *My First Lady III* as preparations were made for the two tours scheduled for the day. Uncle Henry and his crew members were busy loading supplies. The boat captain told himself to focus on getting the boat ready for the first tour, but he couldn't help but think about the second trip later that afternoon. He just hoped things would go as planned.

The first tour went without difficulty, and the crew began preparing for the second one. Uncle Henry made a couple comments to Charlie, his first mate, and then stepped off the boat. Walking up the pier, he pulled out his cell phone and made a call.

When the call was answered, he said, "Okay on this end. Everything okay on yours?"

"So far, so good," Gabbey said. "Just hope the weather holds."

"Me, too," Uncle Henry said. "See you in a few."

The call ended.

. . . . .

Gabbey found Noel outside on the porch deck talking to a table of guests who were having a late breakfast. Bear and Louie were at her side with Noel telling everyone how the two dogs roamed the property and kept the wildlife at bay. She assured everyone there was no danger, but an occasional deer or moose would wander onto the property.

"While we are very cognizant about the safety of our guests," Noel explained, "we are well aware that the wildlife was here before us. The wildlife also adds to the overall atmosphere."

Gabbey waited until Noel was finished then went up to her. "I need to talk to you a minute...Nothing's wrong, at least not here."

The two stepped away from the table. "What's up?" Noel asked with a look of concern.

"Uncle Henry just called and wanted to know if you were available," Gabbey said. "He's short a boat captain as he didn't realize he had booked an overlapping trip with the skiff. He'll take the skiff if you can take *My First Lady III*. He'll be in radio contact and close by all the time, plus you'll have a full crew."

"Why doesn't he let me take the smaller boat?" Noel asked.

"He's about to leave the dock now with that one. *My First Lady III* isn't due to leave for an hour."

Noel hesitated. She'd crewed for him before and had run the boat without him before, but never with a tour on board.

"Weather supposed to be calm and again, he's going to be close by," Gabbey added.

"What about here?" Noel asked.

"You're float manager today. I'll cover you, so go help Henry out." Gabbey added as an afterthought, "I just wish I could go with you."

. . . . .

Noel finished up a couple tasks before going back to her room to change out of her cottage uniform. She made it down to the boat with five minutes to spare.

Charlie, the first mate, was there waiting for her. He helped her aboard and ushered her right into the pilot house. He was a couple years younger than Noel, but much taller and more muscular.

"Thanks for coming on such short notice," he said as Noel stepped behind the wheel. "Captain Henry said to tell you the same. I've already gone through the pre-departure checklist. Engines are running. Temperatures are okay. Oil pressure's the same. Bilge is dry. We fueled up earlier this morning."

It was common for Charlie to do this with Uncle Henry, so Noel had no reason to change the procedure. Besides, she had no doubt Charlie knew the boat better than she did. If something was amiss, he'd let her know.

He continued quickly. "Crew and guests are all onboard. We're ready to get underway as soon as you give the green light, Captain."

He left the pilot house and half-climbed, half-jumped down to the dock. "There's no wind or current to speak of at the moment," he called up. "I suggest I go ahead and take off all the lines and get back on board."

Noel stuck her arm out the door and gave him a thumbs up. As he stepped back into the pilot house a minute later, she said, "Watch the port side and give me a yell when the stern clears."

With the engines in idle, Noel pushed both transmission handles forward. *My First Lady III* edged ahead slowly. When Charlie gave the okay that the stern was clear, she nudged the throttles up as well. They were officially under way.

Charlie moved to stand beside Noel. Giving her a pat on the back, he said, "Nice job. You stay here. I'm going to go check on the guests." As he started to step away, he added, "Captain Henry also said to tell you to take the normal loop. The bald eagles were there this morning."

"Okay," Noel said.

It was a perfect day on the lake. There was a steady gentle breeze coming off the mountain, otherwise there was no wind or current. Noel steered the boat manually at first. As she started to relax, she turned on the auto pilot. She continued to scan the instruments on a regular basis. All remained stable.

She adjusted herself on the seat so she could get a good view of the water ahead as well as keep an eye on all the instruments. She took a sip of the coffee she had brought with her and let out a deep breath. Yes, this was the life. She never regretted her decision to go into the hospitality industry, although oftentimes wondered how it would be to be a full-time waterman. Both professions were hard and seasonal. Gabbey already told her she had a job at the cottage if she wanted it. She was also sure Uncle Henry would use her as needed. Maybe she could continue to do both.

Her thoughts went to Jason. He would be returning to New York soon. In spite of what they had discussed, she wondered about the future of their relationship? Would they…? She cut the thought off, telling herself not to focus on that now, but to enjoy the day, and enjoy what time they had left together this summer.

Just as a wave of sadness threatened to envelope her, Charlie came back into the pilot house. "I'll take over for a while. You go back and mingle with the guests. Several have asked to get a picture with the captain."

"Thanks," Noel said, siding off the chair. "I want to get something more than coffee to drink anyway."

"Take your time," Charlie directed. Noel failed to see the smirk on his face.

Noel straightened her ponytail and pulled her tee shirt down to make it as wrinkled free as possible. She stopped at the bar to get a soda and was surprised to see Bobby there. The two boys were with him as well. They were playing with Bear and Louie, who had come along for the ride.

"What are you doing here?" Bobby said, forcing surprise into his voice. He poured Noel a soda and slid it toward her.

"You didn't know I was here?" Noel said. She reached down and gave each dog a pet. Then she ruffled the hair of the two boys. "Uncle Henry had a conflict. He's out on another tour with the skiff."

"Oh." Bobby refilled Noel's cup after she downed half. "You're the captain, eh?"

Noel nodded. She emptied her cup and set it on the bar. "I should go mingle with the guests."

"Can we come with you?" the boys said simultaneously. The two dogs barked their desire to participate as well.

"I'll have an entourage, eh?" Noel teased.

Noel turned, nodded to the three well-dressed people in line. One was a tall, distinguished looking man. Next to him was a woman of similar height. A younger woman about Noel's age stood next to her.

They watched Noel as she walked away. Then the youngest woman turned to Bobby. "Is that her?"

Bobby nodded. "Yes, it is."

"She's beautiful."

"She is that," Bobby said. He took their drink orders and went to work.

CHAPTER 35

Noel took several steps toward the tables of guests before coming to a sudden stop. Noticing Alex and his wife, she said, "Alex…Maria…what are you guys doing here?" Before they could answer, Noel saw Gabbey standing next to them. "Gabbey!" Noel continued looking around and saw more people she recognized. As a matter of fact, she knew everyone she saw except the man and two women she saw at the bar. She made eye contact with Gabbey again. "What's going on?"

"We're celebrating," Gabbey said.

"Celebrating what?"

Charlie came up behind Noel and gave her a light hug. "Celebrating you taking the boat out the first time with guests on board."

Noel turned and faced him. "Charlie, who's running the boat?"

Uncle Henry's head popped around the corner. "I got it, Noel. You go ahead and have a good time."

Looking back at Charlie, Noel half-demanded, half-pleaded, "Would somebody please tell me what's going on?" She turned to face the crowd. She noticed the room had become quiet. Her hands went up to her mouth when she saw Jason walking toward her, a wide smile across his face. She started to speak as he reached her. His fingers pressed against her lips. He then moved her hands out of the way and gently kissed her.

Jason spoke before she could say anything. "Noel Summers, I have been in love with you from the moment I first saw you. That love has only grown deeper these past weeks. There is no doubt in my mind that I want much more than a summer romance. I want to spend the rest of my life with you." He paused, reaching into his pocket and pulling out a small square box. He dropped down to one knee. "Noel, I love you with all my heart. Will you marry me?"

Noel's hands again went to her mouth as she bent forward. Her eyes started to water. Suddenly, her posture straightened. "My family.... What are they going to say?"

Noel recognized her brother's voice as he approached from the left. Lee stopped beside Jason. "Jason came to visit me at the casino and asked my permission for your hand. We had a long talk. I believe his words are true and that he will care for you in the manner we, your friends and family, would expect. You have my blessing." He gave Noel a hug.

"What about Mother?" Noel said with concern.

A space formed between her brother and Jason. Noel's mother stepped forward. "Jason also came to the reservation and visited me," she said. "You have my blessings, my dear daughter." She gave Noel a hug.

Noel then asked, "What about your parents, Jason? Do they know anything about this?"

Jason pointed to the attractive group at the bar, and Noel realized they must be his family, his parents and twin sister. They were all smiling broadly and nodding their heads.

Noel looked back at Jason, whose eyes had not left her. She took a quick survey of the room. Everyone was watching. Everyone was waiting. She looked down at the box he was holding and was now open. It was the most beautiful diamond engagement ring she had ever seen.

Looking back at Jason who had risen to his feet. Noel spoke softly at first, and then louder with each pronouncement. "Yes…Yes…YES!"

The cheers and applause were loud and sustained. Then the newly engaged couple were mobbed by well-wishers and the celebration began.

Just then, a strong gust of wind struck the port side of the boat, blowing through the windows. The locals looked at one another with widened smiles and nods of their heads. No one spoke, except for Noel's mother who said softly, "The wind gods approve."

"Yes, they do," Lee said. He looked skyward. He laid his arm across his mother's shoulder and gave her a gentle hug. "I think Father approves as well."

. . . . .

The party lasted another two hours. Bobby was kept busy with the help of Cindy at the bar. Staff from the cottage were kept busy keeping the food buffet in order. Freddie and Allen were on their best behavior, helping to clear tables and take care of trash. Bobby had already promised to take them pirate hunting the next full moon.

Not wanting to be left out of the festivities, Bear and

Louie made their rounds as well. Several people asked Noel whether the dogs were going to be in the wedding. Noel replied most definitely. Cindy also kept busy taking photographs. If there was an award for who showed the most excitement, she would win hands down.

Gabbey spent most of her time with Noel's mother and with Jason's parents, learning what it was like to live in New York City. Laura, as sister of the groom-to-be, kept busy answering everybody's questions about Jason. She assured everyone he was indeed what you saw. She also spent time talking to Lee, Noel's brother. No one picked up on their attraction except for Noel and her mother. Mother said to daughter on one occasion, "The wind gods are all around us today."

Jason's mother was anxious to meet everyone, which she did with grace and pride, including spending time with Noel's mother. Noel wondered what they could be talking about, which she mentioned to Jason.

Jason let out a soft chuckle. "They're planning the wedding."

Noel's eyes lit up as this was the first time she had thought that far ahead. "Oh, my."

Jason grabbed her hands as he said, with reassurance, "Don't worry, it will be your day and will be in the tradition you and your family plan and expect."

"But...."

Jason squeezed her hands harder. "I had a conversation with my parents who fully understand your family will want to preserve First Nation marriage traditions. My family is looking forward to learning about your culture." He let go of her hands and gave her a kiss. "My mother did ask whether she could plan an engagement party in New York so you can meet my family and friends."

"I've never been to New York," Noel said cautiously.

Jason smiled. "You'll love it."

Noel pointed toward her mother, who now was talking to Uncle Henry, who had stopped by her table. "My mother hasn't smiled much lately. It's nice to see that again."

"Let's go get my future mother-in-law something to drink. She's the only one not holding a champagne glass," Jason said. "Bobby has got a couple bottles of non-alcoholic bubbly on ice."

Noel's eyes widened. "That's so thoughtful." She kissed Jason on the cheek. As they headed toward the bar, she added, "Can I ask what my mother said when you visited her?"

Jason smiled. "She said that she would be proud to call me her son-in-law." He returned the kiss. "And for the record, my mother told me a couple minutes ago that I would have been a fool not to have asked you."

As they made their way through the crowd, saying hi to everyone and accepting congratulations, Noel did have time to get in, "By the way, I never got a chance to thank you for my ring."

"I'm glad you like it. Your brother told me about a jewelry store near the casino. I was actually surprised at the selection."

Noel admired the ring before looking back at Jason. "When did you have time to plan all this?"

Jason let out another chuckle. "To be truthful, everything

just fell into place. I knew this is how I wanted to propose with both our families and friends around us. And I wanted it to be a surprise."

"Well, it was that," Noel quipped. She grabbed Jason's hand. "Come on, let's get my mother that drink."

. . . . .

Uncle Henry was at the helm of *My First Lady III* as the sun started to drop behind the western side of the lake. The sky remained clear. No rain! The humidity and temperature remained high. No one complained, though, as Bobby kept everyone hydrated and Gabbey's staff kept everyone's appetite satisfied.

As the Baddeck pier came into view, Uncle Henry came out of the pilot house. Spotting Noel talking to a few of the guests, he hollered. "Hey, Noel, you took her out. You want to take her back?"

Noel gave him a wave and headed forward. Bear and Louie were on her heels. The two boys were behind the dogs. Jason started to follow, but Noel waved him away.

"Go spend time with your family."

Docking was no problem with Noel handling the boat masterfully. As everyone disembarked and headed up the pier, Bobby said to Noel and Jason, "You two go on. Cindy and the two boys are going to stay behind and help clean up. You can check on the two newbie bartenders for me, though?"

"No problem," Jason and Noel said in unison as they mingled back with the crowd disembarking.

As they passed Captain Henry and Charlie, who were at the bottom of the gangway. Jason stopped and shook Uncle Henry's hand. He started to say something, but Uncle Henry spoke first.

"Anytime you want to go for a boat ride, you let me know."

Jason smiled. "Don't be surprised if I take you up on that soon as Uncle Andy gets back in town."

Uncle Henry laughed. "He knows he has an open invitation as well."

Noel turned her attention to Charlie. "I wondered why you were so anxious to get me in the pilot house when I first came on board."

Charlie just shrugged as he gave her a hug.

CHAPTER 36

Jason's family decided to extend their stay a couple days. Gabbey put them up in the suites near Jason. Touring the area, Jason's parents certainly understood why Dr. Cunningham had referred Jason to Baddeck. Listening to him play in the evenings only reinforced the point.

Gabbey adjusted the schedules so Noel could spend time with Jason and his family, giving them a partial tour of the Cabot Trail and taking them to the Alexander Graham Bell Museum. She offered to take them on a hike, but Jason's parents declined. Jason's sister, however, jumped at the opportunity.

When they returned from the hike, Noel and Laura walked out onto the deck where Jason was sitting with his parents. The two young women acted like they were becoming best friends.

Laura plopped down onto a chair and grabbed the bottle of water sitting in front of her brother. Emptying half of it, she wiped her mouth and said, "I thought I was in pretty good shape but I'm exhausted." She finished the bottle of water and handed it to Jason. "Take care of your *older* sister… please."

Jason shook his head, saying nothing, as he rose to his feet and headed into the bar.

"So, you had a good time?" Jason's mother asked.

"We had a wonderful time. We took some supplies up to a fire tower manned by college students. It was really cool," Laura said. "This whole place is amazing."

Jason's father nodded and added, "Nothing like I expected."

Laura continued. "Noel is a wonderful host and a wonderful guide." She looked toward the bride-to-be. "She's going to be a wonderful bride, too."

Looking toward Jason's mother, Noel smiled and said, "She's going to help me design my wedding dress. She wants to combine a modern look with the Mi'kmaq heritage. I'm anxious to see what she comes up with."

Jason's mother looked at her daughter. "If there's anyone in the design business that can capture that, it will be Laura. She has an amazing talent for blending various themes into one dress."

"Well, I'm so appreciative of everything she, and everyone else, is doing. It's going to be a wonderful day," Noel said. The excitement left her voice. "Although, we do have a lot to do."

"We have plenty of time to think about that," Jason interrupted. He came up behind Noel with a tray of beverages. He set a couple bottles of water in front of his sister, an iced tea in front of his mother and Noel, and a flight of beer in front of his father. "I know you mainly drink Scotch, Dad, but I thought you might like to try some of the local beers. They're actually quite good."

Beverages served, Jason continued. "What are your guy's plans for tomorrow?"

"We're going up to the First Nation reservation to see Noel's mother and visit the Heritage Center," Laura said. "Mom and I want to see the venue where they're planning the wedding. That may affect the dress design."

"Are you hoping to see anyone else?" Jason asked teasingly.

"I think Lee will be there, too," Laura admitted with a smile.

"I like Lee. He's a good guy," Jason said instead of the tease he had thought of originally.

"One of the first things you two have to do is set a date," Jason's mother said.

Noel's eyebrows rose. Looking at Jason, she said, "We haven't even talked about that yet."

"We'll add it to our list of things to do," Jason said

"The list is getting longer by the minute," Noel bemoaned.

Patting Noel on the arm, Laura said, "Sister, you haven't even started."

Noel looked at Jason, who said, "One thing at a time, my love. One thing at a time."

Jason's father cleared his throat. "With that in mind, can we get some menus? This beer is making me hungry."

. . . . .

"I'm exhausted," Noel said with a sigh as she plopped across Jason's bed. They had just returned from Millbrook where they visited Noel's mother and looked at the venue for the wedding. "My body's crying for sleep, but my mind is going a mile a minute."

Laying down beside her, Jason said, "All you need is to

remember is how much I love you and how happy we are." He rolled toward her, draping his arm across her chest. He kissed her lightly on the lips.

"It's just a lot to think about…a lot to plan," Noel complained.

"Don't worry about the planning. It'll get done. My sister will see to that, and I suspect you have some friends that'll join her."

"You're right about that," Noel said. "But still…."

"Don't worry. It'll all come together. You'll be a beautiful bride, and it will be a beautiful day."

"I was worried about what your parents would think about the Heritage Center. It's not fancy or elegant or anything like that."

"Laura thought it was perfect, especially with your brother being there." Jason let out a laugh before continuing. "My mother took a little time before she eventually saw what my sister saw. My father will be happy as long as everyone else is happy and he has a corner to stand in to watch."

Noel tapped Jason's arm. "Your father's a smart man. You're a lot like him."

Jason laughed again. "I've learned a lot from my father. I'm going to stand back and stay out of the way as well."

"It's your day, too," Noel reminded.

"Yes, it is," Jason agreed. "And my goal that day is to make you as happy as possible."

Noel kissed him again. "We haven't set a date yet."

"Your mother thought sometime next spring. She said that's when the area was the most beautiful," Jason said.

"That'll give us about nine months to plan. Plus, I should have a feel about my career, and you'll be finished school and should have an idea what you're going to do."

"Like I told you before, Gabbey has offered me a position here as assistant manager. She's offered Cindy a similar position."

Jason hesitated. "You know, Noel, neither one of us has to work."

"Your sister explained all that to me when we were hiking," Noel said. "She doesn't have to work either, but it sounds like she works as hard as your mother and father."

"She does."

"And you're working hard on your career." Noel pushed a strand of hair from her face. "I want an opportunity to work on mine as well. My mother instilled in me the need as a woman to be financially independent."

"Okay then, so, you agree with sometime next spring," Jason said.

"If you think that's enough time to get everything done."

Jason shrugged. "We'll make it work."

"We just need to pick a specific date," Noel said. She kissed him hard on the lips. She started to repeat the gesture when she suddenly said, "Where are we going to live?"

Jason sat up. "Uncle Andy called me earlier to congratulate us while you and my sister were out shopping. Gabbey had called him. He was very excited and wished us well. He evidently owns several properties in and around town, including the house next door to him. It's presently vacant. He's offered this to us as a wedding present."

"To rent? That's very kind of him," Noel said.

"No, he wants to give it to us.

"*Giving* us the house?"

"That's what he said."

Noel didn't know what to say at first. Recovering, she explained, "He and his wife used to host wonderful parties there. I'd want to do some updating, but overall, it's a beautiful home just like the one he lives in."

"It's a place to start," Jason pointed out.

"He's just giving it to us?"

Jason let out a chuckle. "Uncle Andy did say he wouldn't mind having me nearby, so he'd have somebody to go to lunch with once in a while."

"You two are something else, you know that?" Noel said.

CHAPTER 37

The staff of the Baddeck Cottage refocused on the tourists that continued to stream into the area in near-record numbers. The weather continued to be hot with an occasional afternoon thunderstorm. With the heat, there was an underlying concern about forest fires, especially with the area's experience a couple years before. Those in the local fire tower remained on high alert. Noel and other volunteers continued to ensure the fire tower was well supplied.

The cottage continued to bustle with activity, with Noel and the rest of the staff putting in long hours. Except for accompanying Noel on an occasional fire tower run, Jason stayed out of the way, spending his time practicing. Uncle Andy stopped by occasionally, usually right around lunch time, to check on Jason's progress. The maestro was pleased with the young pianist's progress.

During this time, yet another idea began to surface for Uncle Andy. The more he heard Jason play, the more he thought the idea a possibility. He called his dear friend Joseph Cunningham, who was hesitant at first until he realized the significance of what it would have for everyone, and for the school as a whole. It would take some rescheduling on Uncle Andy's part as well as Jason returning to New York early. Dr. Cunningham signed off on the idea. All Uncle Andy had to do was discuss it with Jason.

During what would be their last lunch together for the summer, Uncle Andy tossed the idea out to Jason. The young pianist's reaction was what the maestro predicted. "Are you serious?"

"I think you know me enough by now, Jason, to realize that I would never joke about something like this," Uncle Andy said. "It's an opportunity for you, and for the school. And I have already spoken to Dr. Cunningham, who is supportive of the idea."

"Damn!"

. . . . .

Around midnight, Noel made her way to the dining area. She heard the piano as she turned the corner. She stopped at the three steps that led up to the lounge and bar areas. She had no doubt that her fiancé was phenomenal. She instinctively rolled the engagement ring around her finger before looking down at it. A single two-caret, heart-shaped diamond surrounded by small rubies sparkled back at her. A warmth lasered through her body.

Noel slid up on a barstool, mouthing *water* as one of the new bartenders approached. When it was delivered, she took a long swallow before turning to listen. She recognized it as the Beethoven piece Jason was preparing for the recital. The more time she spent around Jason, the more she learned about music.

Jason finished a short time later and acknowledged the scattered applause. He announced he was finished for the evening, thanked everyone for listening and thanked everyone for their contributions to the tip jar

Setting the jar on the bar, he kissed Noel on the cheek. "How long have you been here?"

"Actually, not that long," Noel admitted.

"I'm glad you're here. We need to talk about a change in my schedule."

Noel's eyes widened. Before anything else could be said, the bartender came up to make sure they didn't need anything before she left. Noel was okay. Jason asked for water. When she returned, Jason slid the tip jar toward her.

"This is for you and the other servers who worked tonight," he said. "I trust you'll divide it up fairly."

"For real?" the girl said, looking at the jar. She looked at Noel.

Noel pointed to the jar. "Jason does that every night. It's okay."

The girl looked like she was going to cry. "Thank you so much," she stammered.

Noel waved her arm down the bar. "Now go close out so you can go home and get some rest. You're here tomorrow night, too, right?"

The girls nodded. "Thank you again," she said as she took the jar along with her own tip bucket. She almost forgot the cash register drawer but hurried back for that.

Noel turned to Jason and said, *"A change in schedule?"*

Jason leaned forward and gave her a kiss. Then he told her about his lunch with Uncle Andy.

CHAPTER 38

Six Weeks Later
New York City

Jason had always had a bit of nerves when he performed before faculty and his peers at school. That feeling had dissipated over the summer when he was in Baddeck. Now, instead of nervous, he was excited. His master's recital was about to begin. Get through this, and he would have completed all the requirements, including the two papers, to graduate from Barrett Conservatory of Music.

The faculty panel, seven in total, were already in their chairs. The auditorium was filling fast. His parents and Noel were in their reserved seats off to the left. Next to them were his sister and Lee.

The stage crew was finishing their preparations. Jason's final glance was at the grand piano sitting center stage in front of the curtain. Beauty was his favorite piano, the one from Dr. Cunningham's studio. He had talked to it earlier that morning, saying, "I'll show you off, Beauty, if you show me off."

The stage manager, an undergraduate piano student, tapped Jason on the shoulder. Holding up five fingers, he said, "Five minutes. Jason." He hesitated. "Go be our hero."

Jason gave the younger man a smile and shook the offered hand. The stage manager then made sure Jason's tuxedo was in order, bow tie properly aligned and hair combed.

Dr. Cunningham, also dressed in a smart-looking tux, came up and gave Jason a pat on the shoulder followed by a one-arm hug. It surprised Jason, as the man wasn't known for any sort of personal contact. Jason figured today was different. This was important for the teacher as well as the student.

"Take a couple deep breaths," Cunningham directed. "Your progress over the summer has been amazing. Now go show everyone what you can do."

He gave Jason another pat. The house lights dimmed, and Dr. Cunningham walked out on stage to introduce Jason.

Forty-three minutes later, the last notes of the last selection, a condensed version of Tchaikovsky's Piano Concerto No. 1, were played. Dr. Cunningham and Jason chose this piece to end the recital because it was powerful and showed the pianist's technical as well as interpretive talents. There was another reason it was selected which would become apparent shortly.

The piece ended with a flare. Jason dropped his hands to his knees. He bowed his head and closed his eyes. A sense of calm enveloped him. He took a couple deep breaths. He opened his eyes, rose to his feet, and turned toward the audience. The audience burst into applause. Whistles and cheers were added by the student section. It wasn't long before the entire audience was on their feet. There was even applause coming from behind the curtain that had remained closed during the performance. Jason stood there somewhat stunned. The applause continued. He took several deep bows before pointing to the piano to acknowledge its participation in the performance.

Yes, Beauty had performed well.

Jason bowed again and then walked off stage. The applause and cheering continued. Dr. Cunningham and others were waiting for him. The stage manager handed him a towel and a bottle of water. Joseph Cunningham was all smiles, a rarity in itself. That he gave Jason another one-arm hug added to the aura. He put both arms on the pianist's shoulders and looked him hard in the eyes.

"That, Mr. Kinde, was the finest masters recitals I have ever witnessed. Well done. Congratulations!"

"I hope the panel agrees with you," Jason said, daring a quick glance in that direction.

"I don't think there'll be an issue. Now for your encore."

Pulling in a deep breath, Jason said with conviction, "Let's do it,"

Dr. Cunningham nodded.

Under normal circumstances, the student would return to the stage, take a bow and then perform an encore. However, tonight was not going to be a normal encore. Dr. Cunningham walked out on stage instead. There were murmurs throughout as the audience realized something different was about to happen.

Dr. Cunningham waited for the noise level to subside, then spoke into the microphone he carried with him. "I must say, that was quite a recital from Mr. Kinde." More applause followed. "Now is the time Jason would normally come out for an encore." The professor held up his hands as the student section started to cheer. Continuing to look at the enthusiastic group, he said, "That's going to happen in a moment. However, there's going to be a variation from the norm.

"Mr. Kinde began his recital with Beethoven's first piano concerto. He ended with Tchaikovsky's first piano concerto. We are going to continue with the theme of firsts today. Mr. Kinde's encore is going to be performed with the school's full orchestra. That is a first for a masters recital.

"As many of you are aware, Jason has been away for the summer, secluded in the mountains of Nova Scotia, Canada. When the idea for him to play with the orchestra came about, he returned a couple weeks earlier than planned and has been rehearsing with our orchestra diligently since. The piece to be presented is a premier work by the world-renowned composer/conductor, Andrew Summers. The piece is entitled Piano Concerto #1 in G Minor.

"Ladies and gentlemen, Mr. Jason Kinde, accompanied by the Barrett Symphonic Orchestra, to be conducted by the composer himself, the esteemed Andrew Summers."

The curtains opened to show the student orchestra already seated. Jason walked out on stage along with Andrew Summers. They each shook hands with the first violinist and then turned to face the audience. Loud applause followed. Andrew Summers stepped up to the podium as Jason took his seat at the piano. Seat adjusted, Jason gave the conductor a nod. A moment later, the first notes of Andrew Summers' Piano Concerto # 1 were heard.

It started softly, a moonlit starry night. Footsteps on the

pavement. A gentle breeze. Footsteps continued. The pace increased. There was a gust of wind, and the piano could be heard. The concerto continued.

Midway through the second movement, the wind suddenly increased. The percussion section became prominent, augmented by strong piano passages. It was the loudest section of the concerto. Just as suddenly, the wind died. The music continued. Fourteen minutes later, Jason and the orchestra finished with a flare.

And then it was over. The nighttime stroll through Baddeck was finished. The pirates had escaped yet again. The sun was rising over the town.

There was a moment of silence as the audience digested what they had just heard. Then as one voice, there was thunderous applause as everyone rose to their feet. Andrew Summers turned and faced the crowd. He bowed and motioned to Jason who had also risen to his feet. The conductor was smiling as he acknowledged the orchestra with applause himself. Jason wore a stunned expression.

They had been rehearsing the piece for the past three weeks. During the last rehearsal, Uncle Andy commented on how energetic the students were in their playing. However, nothing prepared the maestro for what it sounded like today. Today, it was....

He would later describe it as *majestic*.

The conductor stepped off the podium and stood beside Jason, leading the crowd in applause. The entire orchestra were also on their feet clapping. Jason stepped over to the first violinist to shake her hand. She then pulled him in for a hug.

"That's from all of us," she said. "Thank you."

"No, thank you," Jason insisted. He looked up and scanned the entire stage. "All of you were terrific," he said. He then acknowledged the orchestra with hands held high and wide.

Jason moved back to stand beside Uncle Andy. The applause continued. The crowd wanted a second encore. The first violinist rose to her feet and stepped forward. She was a senior violin student who was also studying conducting.

She took the microphone the stage manager handed her and spoke. "We wanted to do something to thank Mr. Summers for spending the past three weeks with us rehearsing for Mr. Kinde's recital. While it is indeed Jason's day, it has also been an opportunity for the members of the orchestra to work and perform with Mr. Summers." Her attention turned to the maestro. "So as a way of thanking you, we have prepared a little something especially for you."

With a perplexed yet curious look on his face, Andrew Summers stepped off to the side next to Dr. Cunningham. The two men looked at one another, indicating neither knew what was about to happen. Cunningham thought about stopping the students when Uncle Andy laid his hand on his arm to hold him in place.

"Relax, Joseph, I'm sure whatever it is will be wonderful."

Jason moved to the piano. The violinist took the podium to become the conductor. She opened a score of music she had carried with her. Conductor and pianist nodded to one another. The music began.

The audience was treated to a medley of Andrew

Summers' show tunes, arranged, and played by students at Barrett. While Jason was an active participant, the focus was on the orchestra as a whole, with many students getting short solos.

In the end, the audience was again on their feet. Andrew Summers came back on stage and gave the conductor a hug.

"That was wonderful. Thank you." More applause followed.

As Jason stood next to the two conductors, one young, one old, he stole a glance down to his family. They were on their feet with everyone else. His mother, Noel, and his sister were all three crying. His father had a wide smile on his face. Lee was clapping as well and gave him two thumbs up.

Jason's eyes then moved to where the judges were seated. The man farthest to the left, who was the chairman of the masters committee and also the school's president, met Jason's gaze. He smiled ever so slightly and gave the young pianist a positive nod.

CHAPTER 39

The hotel adjacent to the school was where Jason's parents sponsored the post-recital reception. Jason was surrounded by fellow students who were anxious to offer their congratulations. Jason was careful to acknowledge and thank those in the orchestra for their participation. Faculty and others waited their turn to give their congratulations as well. Dr. Cunningham continued to praise Jason's performance, extending his comments to the orchestra. He was especially excited as Jason Kinde was his first student to complete the masters level program in two years.

The conservatory's president came up to congratulate Jason and say how pleased he was at everyone's performance. Not known for mincing words, he was quick to critique Andrew Summer's concerto as an exceptional work.

"I am sure the concerto will become very popular very quickly. Your performance, Jason, certainly made its premier memorable." He then pulled two envelopes from his suit pocket and handed them to the young pianist.

Jason took the envelopes. "Should I open them here?"

"You can, or I can tell you what they contain, and you can read them through later."

Jason looked at his family who were standing beside him. Uncle Andy and Dr. Cunningham stepped up to them as well.

Pointing to the school's president, who was an old friend, Uncle Andy said, "He's chomping at the bit to tell you."

Jason nodded and the man spoke. "The first envelope contains the official letter announcing you have been awarded a masters degree in Piano Performance. You can pick up your diploma in my office anytime. And yes, I had this prepared ahead of time in anticipation of your performance today."

"Thank you, sir," Jason said, shaking the man's hand as he fought back tears.

The president continued. "The second letter is a formal offer from the school for you to come on board as a part-time assistant professor with full benefits, specific duties yet to be determined. The part-time status is included to give you plenty of freedom to pursue whatever the future holds for you as a concert pianist. Again, I did the letter in advance." As he again shook Jason's hand, he added, "Off the record, Mr. Kinde, we can convert the part-time component to full-time anytime you choose."

There were more handshakes and hugs all around. When it was Noel's turn, she kissed him on the cheek and said, "I'm so proud of you and so glad you came to Baddeck."

Jason kissed her back. "I am, too."

Seeing that her brother didn't know what to do with the envelopes, Laura reached out and took them from him. "I'll take these for safe keeping. You go on and enjoy the party."

"Good idea, Laura," Uncle Andy said. He took Jason by the arm. "If you all will excuse us, I have someone I want Jason to meet."

The duo worked their way through the crowd toward

the bar. There were additional handshakes and offers of congratulations. Jason took it all in with gratitude and humility, always making sure he pointed out the man next to him as the one who actually made it all possible. He used a popular quote that hung above a doorway at school: *There is no musician without music.*

They made it to the bar, Uncle Andy grabbing a flute of champagne and Jason asking for a bottle of water. A tall, thin, distinguished man in an expensive-looking suit came up to them. Holding his own glass of champagne up in a toast, he said, "Well, Andrew, you certainly lived up to your reputation. I am sure the concerto will climb in popularity rather quickly." The man looked towards Jason. "As for you, Mr. Kinde, congratulations." He held out his hand. "William Gregory, Andrew's agent. I know we have spoken on the phone, but it's a pleasure to finally meet you in person. An exceptional performance all around. I especially liked the concept of performing various composers' number ones."

"I am happy you were able to come and am glad you enjoyed it," Jason said.

"That I did, young man. That I did." He took a swallow of his champagne. "What are your plans now that you've completed the program here at Barrett?"

Jason struggled with what to say.

Thankfully, Uncle Andy stepped in. "You know, he has no plans as of yet."

"I have a faculty position at the school," Jason injected.

"That you do," Uncle Andy said. "But Mr. Gregory is talking about plans as a performer."

The agent emptied his glass and held it forward for a refill. "Fair enough." He took a sip of the new drink. "I'm prepared to offer my firm's services as your agent and any other way we may be of assistance. We do this for Mr. Summers, and he has been quite pleased with us over the years. Isn't that correct, Andrew?"

"I wouldn't be bringing Jason to you if I wasn't," Uncle Andy said, half joking, half serious.

"You're one of the biggest entertainment agencies in the country," Jason pointed out. "Why are you interested in me?"

The agent took a long swallow of the champagne that had been refreshed. "Many years ago, my father, who founded the firm, and Andrew were standing having a similar conversation. Andrew had just completed his studies at Peabody in Baltimore. One of the greatest assets my father had was the ability to assess talent, especially young talent. I will tell you the same thing he told Andrew that day. There are many talented musicians in the world seeking fame and fortune. The competition is fierce. We as a talent agency have to weed through these masses to find those that stand out from all the others. My father thought Andrew Summers was one of those, and he was correct. I feel the same way about you, Jason." He paused for another sip of champagne. "You are one of the finest *young* pianists I have ever heard."

Jason found himself speechless yet again.

The agent continued. "I'm going to send you a letter of intent and a contract for you to review. I'll send it to you through the school if that's okay." Jason nodded that it was. "Review it carefully. I would also have an entertainment attorney review it as well."

"I thought you were going to be my attorney," Jason said.

"Once you sign the final documents, I can be. Until then, you need to make sure I am who and what you want."

Jason started to protest, but the agent held up his hand. "If I was your agent, this is exactly what I would advise you to do."

"Whoever you choose to work with in that capacity is going to control your life. You need to be comfortable with that person before you sign on the bottom line," Uncle Andy said.

"Sounds like good advice to me," Jason said.

THE FINAL MOVEMENT

Baddeck, Canada
Before Christmas

Gabbey leaned over the counter to look at the registration computer. The Baddeck Cottage was booked solidly for the night and the next two days, not an uncommon occurrence on the weekend of the cottage's annual Holiday Celebration. Depending on what day Christmas fell, the event was scheduled either one or two weekends before the holiday. The party had started a decade ago as an open house for the locals, but each year, more and more tourists migrated to Baddeck for the event. It was an economic benefit for the entire community during a time when the tourist trade was minimal. Unlike some communities, Baddeck never complained about the tourists, always welcoming them with open arms. College students saw the weekend as an opportunity to work during the winter break. It also gave them a foot in the door for summer jobs.

"We're at capacity, which is good, but we have no room for anyone who might come in without a reservation," Gabbey explained.

"We have those suites on the top floor we can use if necessary. Also, the room where Jason stayed during the summer is open," Noel pointed out. She couldn't avoid a hint of sadness in her voice.

Gabbey started to say something but caught herself in time. She took a quick look at Cindy who gave her a wink.

Before anything else could be said, Uncle Henry walked through the doors and stepped into the lobby.

Giving all three a flirty look, he said, "My, my, my, don't you ladies look beautiful this evening, all decked out in your holiday dresses."

"You look dapper yourself." Gabbey teased. The boat captain was dressed in khaki pants, white shirt with a Santa tie, and a blue blazer.

Everyone laughed. Uncle Henry gave each a kiss on the cheek. Taking a look around the lobby, he said, "The cottage has certainly outdone itself this year. The outside looks spectacular. With all the lights and decorations, you can see the place from the harbor. It looks fabulous inside as well."

"Go on in and take a look around," Gabbey said, motioning toward the dining area. "The bar's open, food's out. Help yourself."

"Just save me a little champagne," Cindy teased, having been told it was the only night of the year Uncle Henry consumed any alcohol.

"I'm sure Bobby already has you covered," Uncle Henry said with a wink.

As he started to step way, the boat captain said, "Seriously, do you ladies need anything or want something to drink?"

"No, but thanks," Noel said. "Maybe when Santa arrives, I'll have a glass."

"I'll see that that happens." Uncle Henry nodded at Gabbey as he handed her a set of keys. "Here's the keys to the van. I parked it out back in the far corner. That was the only space left." He turned and headed toward the party.

"What was Uncle Henry doing with the van?" Noel asked, confused.

"He made an airport run for me," Gabbey said. "Everybody was busy, so he volunteered,"

Before Noel could say anything else, the front doors opened and in walked Laura and her parents. Noel saw them and her eyes widened. "Laura…Mr. and Mrs. Kinde! I didn't know you guys were coming?"

Laura stepped forward to give Noel a hug. "This is an open house, isn't it?"

"Why yes," Noel stammered as she greeted Laura's parents. "What a wonderful surprise."

"It's Laura's Christmas present to us," Mrs. Kinde said. "She knew how much her father and I enjoyed the time here this summer, so she thought it would be fun to visit in the winter."

Noel looked at Cindy who had a smirk on her face. "You knew about this didn't you?" Noel demanded gently. "That's why the overflow rooms upstairs are empty."

Cindy shrugged. "You never know who's going to walk through the door."

Gabbey greeted Jason's family. "Come on in. We'll get your luggage taken care of." She pointed to the dining room area. "Bar's open. Food's out."

"Wait a minute, how did you all get here?" Noel said.

"Henry, the boat captain, picked us up at the airport," Mr. Kinde said.

Noel looked at Gabbey. "You all knew about this, too, didn't you?" Before anyone could answer, Noel's expression turned mournful. "Is Jason here?"

"He's with Uncle Andy trying to line up performance venues," Laura said solemnly.

Just then, Uncle Andy came around the corner from the back. "And we got a few concerts already lined up, including two performances in Paris." He pointed to Laura. "I expect to see some fancy dresses there, too."

"Oh, you will," the young designer said.

Noel gave the man a hug and accepted a kiss on the cheek. "How did you get here?"

"I hitched a ride with these guys," Uncle Andy said. "Actually, we were on the same flight."

"That was nice," Noel said, trying but failing to keep the sadness from her voice. They were all here except Jason. "Wait a minute," she said suddenly. "You said we came on the same fight. Plus, you're here?" She stared at the conductor standing across from her. Just then, there was applause coming from the lounge, starting out softly and growing rapidly. Then there was music. Someone was playing the piano.

With little hesitation, Noel dashed toward the sound.

The area was crowded so she had to slow her pace. When she finally got close enough to see the piano, she stopped. There was Jason sitting at the piano playing Christmas tunes. He was dressed in a dark blue suit and Christmas tie. He had a red and white pointy Christmas hat plopped atop his head.

Bear and Louie laid on the floor beside the bench, each with their own holiday sweater. They all three looked silly, but Noel didn't care. Her wish for the night had come true. Jason turned her way, spotting her in the crowd. She gave him a petite wave. He returned with a wide smile.

The music continued.

As she stood and listened to the music, there was a tap on her shoulder. She turned to see Uncle Henry standing next to her, two glasses of champagne in his hand. Handing one to Noel and holding his up in a toast, he said, "Merry Christmas."

Noel took the drink. Gently clicking glasses, she said, "Merry Christmas to you."

"I told you I'd bring you a drink tonight when Santa Clause arrived," Uncle Henry said.

"Thank you," Noel said, taking a sip. She then gave him a hug. "Thank you for delivering him."

The party lasted until midnight when the predicted snow arrived. The forecast called for one to two inches. Locals knew better and warned everyone to get their high-top boots ready. "When the storm comes over the mountain, she usually comes with a load."

Uncle Henry bid everyone goodnight, wanting to get home before too much accumulated. He lived several miles out of town. Jason's parents went to their room a short time later. Gabbey helped close out the kitchen so the crew could get home before the weather got too bad. Bobby sent the newbie bartenders home, saying he'd close out the bar. Cindy said she would help, too.

"Naturally," Noel teased.

Laura and Uncle Andy worked on finishing off the last bottle of champagne. Noel and Jason worked on several bottles of water.

Bear and Louie heard the word "snow" and made a bee line for the door. Noel usually didn't let them out this late, but knew they'd pester her until they had a chance to check the weather. Louie liked snow as long as it wasn't too deep, and Bear liked the snow regardless.

Everyone commented on how well the party went off.

"Now, you have to have two parties every year," Laura said.

"Two?" Noel queried.

"Yeah, this one and the summer picnic," Laura quipped. "I heard that one was spectacular, too."

"Thank you," Noel said. She looked at Uncle Andy and then at Jason. "And Santa Clause made it as well."

"We thought you would like that," Cindy said.

"I did," Noel said. "I really did." She ran her arm through Jason's and gave him a quick kiss. "And thank you, Jason, not only for coming tonight, but for entertaining everyone."

"Glad I was able to do it," Jason said. He let out a soft chuckle as he pointed to the tip jar sitting on the bar. "Looks like my biggest tip night ever." He slid the jar toward Bobby.

"What's everyone doing tomorrow?" Noel asked, looking at Jason. She was afraid of the answer.

"My parents have a late afternoon flight back to New York," Laura said. "The storm is supposed to pass through quickly, so they should be okay…assuming they can get to the airport."

"I can take them in the Jeep," Noel said.

"I'll need a ride, too," Uncle Andy said. "We're on the same flight again."

"What about you, Laura?" Noel asked.

Laura pointed toward Cindy and Bobby. "I'm going with them to the casino."

"The casino where my brother works?" Noel said.

"That's the only casino I know around here," Bobby said with a smirky grin.

Noel stared at Laura who quickly explained. "He invited me to visit for a few days. Then we're going to spend Christmas with your mother."

"That'll be great," Noel said. "I'll be driving up Christmas Eve. Gabbey gave me Christmas off."

"Bobby and I will be back in town, so we got the place covered," Cindy added.

There was a moment's silence as Noel's gaze slowly went to Jason. "And you?"

"Uncle Andy and I have a New Year's Eve concert in New York. We're going to premiere his concerto to the general public."

"I saw the reviews online," Cindy said. "They were very favorable."

"We didn't know the press would be attending the recital," Uncle Andy said. "Evidently my agent sent out a press release."

"I'm glad I didn't know," Jason said.

Laura spoke next. "The write ups didn't do the performance justice. You and the orchestra were terrific." She gave

Uncle Andy a gentle poke in the arm. "That includes you, too, sir."

"Let me ask you this, Uncle Andy," Bobby said. "What is the actual role of the conductor, anyway?"

"I just wave a stick around," the conductor said. He emptied his glass of champagne and held it out to Laura for a refill.

Jason frowned as he said, "The conductor serves as the messenger between the composer and musicians. He or she controls all aspects of the performance."

"I can understand that," Bobby said, as he worked on opening another bottle of champagne.

Noel focused her attention back on Jason. "So, you have to go back and rehearse?"

"I have to practice, yes, but we won't start working with the orchestra until two days before New Year's Eve."

"Soo…?" Noel crooned.

Jason answered quickly. "Gabbey said I can hang out here and practice if I want."

"And?"

Jason gave her a hug. "I'd be honored to be invited to your mother's for Christmas dinner."

Noel returned the hug with a kiss. "Of course you're invited."

The new bottle of bubbly was poured. The curtains to the patio had been left open. The deck lights were still on. There was already an inch plus of snow on the ground. The rate of fall was hard to determine, however, as the wind continued to swirl as it came off the mountain. Jason commented that it was a Christmas Card scene, which stimulated Cindy's interest. She grabbed her phone and dragged Bobby outside to try and capture the image.

"What about a coat?" Uncle Andy called out.

"Bobby'll keep me warm," Cindy chirped.

Laura made sure everyone's glass was capped off. Setting the bottle down, she said, "To be honest, Uncle Andy, I was curious how people around here would react to the concerto. I'm glad they responded the way they did."

Jason had played the piece earlier in the evening, and it was a huge success.

"Populations may differ, but people everywhere enjoy classical music," Uncle Andy said. "People around here have always been supportive of me, of my music, as well as maintaining my privacy."

"I have a question," Noel said. "Besides the numbering… concerto # 1…isn't it common for a musical piece like yours to have a name?"

Uncle Andy took a sip of champagne. "Jason and I were talking about that on the flight to Halifax. I said I would name it when I found one I liked, one that captures the essence of the piece. Just before we landed, Jason said he had an idea. Right, Jason?"

Jason nodded. "I'm working on it."

THE ENCORE

When the last drop of champagne was finished, everyone left, leaving Noel and Jason alone at the bar. "Want something stronger than water?" Noel offered.

"I'm okay. You?"

"I'm fine, thanks."

While Jason went behind the bar for more water, Noel grabbed the only two coats left on the coat rack. Taking one of the waters and handing Jason his coat, she said, "Let's go outside a few minutes."

They went out through the patio doors and walked up to the rail. The grounds were now totally covered in white. Lights from the town sparkled as the snow continued to fall at a moderate rate. For the moment, there was no wind. It was indeed a picturesque sight. They absorbed the view in silence a few moments, each with their own thoughts.

Noel leaned into Jason and put her arm through his. "Christmas came early for me this year," she said. "You surprised me and came to the party." They kissed.

Jason said, "I told Uncle Andy I really wanted to be here tonight. He said he did, too. Luckily, it worked out."

"So, you've got a concert lined up for New Year's Eve?" Noel said. "That's exciting."

"Believe it or not, it's sold out."

"Wow!"

"But..." Jason gave her a hug. "I have tickets for you and the family."

"That's so nice," Noel said. "I love you, Jason Kinde."

"And I love you, Noel Summers."

They kissed again

"Plus, you're going to Paris," Noel said.

"Two concerts so far. Uncle Andy said there'll probably be more. His agent..." Jason paused. "*Our* agent thinks Uncle Andy's concerto will be in high demand."

"With you as the soloist?" Noel asked hesitantly.

"Uncle Andy told me he can control that somewhat, but that may depend on the venue," Jason explained. "Plus, you want other pianists and orchestras to start playing the concerto as well,"

"Regardless, your career is taking off," Noel said.

"It's a start," Jason shrugged, "but let's talk about us."

Noel nodded.

"Everyone likes the idea of a spring wedding. We just have to pick a specific date. I'll block out time so we can go on a honeymoon. In the meantime, I'll start my performance career. You'll work here at the cottage. We can work together on getting the house ready. I'll get back here anytime I can, and you can join me on the road anytime you can."

The conversation was interrupted by the barking and arrival of Bear and Louie as they came up the steps onto the patio. Both were short of breath. Both were covered in snow. They shook out their fur, and after getting a couple pets, plopped down at the couple's feet while Jason and Noel continued to plan their next few months.

They kissed. The snow continued. Time stood still.

"Before he started having problems, my father and mother used to go outside during the first snowfall," Noel finally said. "When we were old enough, they took us out as well. My mother said it was a way to remember we were all a part of something much bigger than ourselves."

"Then let's make tonight the start of our first tradition," Jason said.

"That'll be nice," Noel said.

A couple gusts of wind went by. Noel shivered slightly.

"You cold?" Jason said.

"A little."

"Then let's go inside. I'll warm you up."

Noel smiled and took one last look at the scene before her. *Yes, we are all part of something much bigger than ourselves,* she thought. *But at this particular moment, all I see is Jason, and all he sees is me. I hope you understand, Mother.*

As she started to turn, another thought crossed Noel's mind. Aloud, she said, "Jason, what was the name you were thinking about for Uncle Andy's concerto."

Jason turned and took Noel in his arms. He looked out across the snow. Just as he started to speak, another gust of wind blew by.

When it passed, he spoke softly, *"The Winds of Baddeck."*

NOTE FROM THE AUTHOR

Thank you for choosing *The Winds Of Baddeck.* I hope you enjoyed reading it as much as I enjoyed writing it. Please consider leaving a review on Amazon or another platform. Your review is very valuable. If you wish to contact me directly, you can email me at dorseybutter6@aol.com. I am always happy to hear from readers.

Thank you to my wife Suzanne for her continued support and tireless editing as the manuscript progressed. Thank you to Caroline Ailanthus for the final edit and comments. And thanks to all the beta readers who took the time to review and critique the work. Lastly, thanks to Salt Water Media for their production work on this book. I greatly appreciate everyone's efforts to help make the story enjoyable to read!

- D.

www.ingramcontent.com/pod-product-compliance
Lightning Source LLC
Chambersburg PA
CBHW050925030726
47503CB00007BB/2478
* 9 7 8 1 6 2 8 0 6 4 6 7 4 *